COLD MOON

The Witches of Langstone Bay

JOANNE MALLORY

Lighthouse Press
www.lighthousepress.co.uk

Cold Moon
The Witches of Langstone Bay, Book 3

Lighthouse Press
www.lighthousepress.co.uk

Cover design - Mallory's Book Covers

For Dad.

For my readers and friends who have waited so patiently for me to get this book finished. It's been a hell of a year.

PROLOGUE

AUGUST 2010

ELLIE TRACED her finger across the dates on the calendar.

It seemed the summer had crept by without her noticing. She had to be back at uni on Tuesday for the start of the new semester.

Two more days.

She looked around her bedroom. She'd arrived home for the summer a few weeks ago, and it'd felt strange being back in this little room, in her parents' house, after living in dorms in London for the last year.

The tide was in, and the calm evening soothed the water, as it would normally soothe her. But not today; restless agitation bounced through her, and she knew only one thing would help.

Opening the small casement window, she watched the waves softly lap the decking that surrounded the west side of Mill House. The sun caught the auburn streaks in her Mum's hair as she tended her pot plants.

As Ellie watched her, she stilled, turning to look up, smiling. "Alright?"

Pushing the window open further, she leaned out. "Mum, I'm going to take the boat out for a couple of hours."

Judy nodded, giving her a wave. "Okay, be careful."

Latching the window, Ellie picked up her baseball cap, pulling her ponytail through it as she went downstairs and out the back door.

The early evening sun warmed the soft cotton of her t-shirt, and she breathed deeply, savouring the salty air.

The gravel crunched beneath the soft soles of her deck shoes, as she walked through her Mum's beloved garden.

Lupins and foxgloves littered the flower beds; a haven for bees and ladybirds. Ellie touched their soft petals as she went, following the meandering path that led down to the water.

The motor boat bobbed with the surf at the end of the short quay, and she stopped for a minute to smile at her.

The little craft was a sanity saver, and Ellie couldn't be more grateful that her parents understood her need to be on the water.

Climbing aboard, she secured the lines, letting herself absorb the lift and swell of the ocean beneath her feet.

The inboard purred to life, courtesy of her Dad's dab hand, and she steered the craft out into the quiet bay. Briefly closing her eyes she took in another lungful of the sweet, summery air and let the scent of the ocean wrap around her.

She'd pack up tomorrow, get ready to head back to London.

She steeled herself against the sadness that dropped through her.

"I love London." She frowned as the words left her lips. She sounded belligerent, even to her own ears. "I bloody do love London."

And she did—on one level. She loved the people, the fast pace. Uni and her friends, her job at the wellness centre...

Smoothing her palms round the chrome wheel she searched for other things she loved about it, finally giving up. It wasn't that she hated it.

But living in London wasn't living here.

This was her home: the bay, the Island. She belonged here. And she'd always known it.

Going to uni in the city was for the best, she knew that too, but *knowing it* didn't make it any easier.

She walked herself through all the reasons why she knew it was right: she had to stretch herself, see new things, live on her own. It was an excellent university...

Rolling her blue eyes, she sighed. How many times did she have to go through repeating her reasons back to herself? Uni was only four years, and she'd already finished the first. She came home—often. She was only an hour away. She just had to woman-up and get on with it.

Fate had been poking her for some time, forcing her out of her comfort zone, and this was just another shove to get her where she needed to be. After all, Ellie knew there must've been some universal interference for her to even apply to King's College in the first place.

Giving herself a shake, she straightened up at the wheel. Throwing her shoulders back and lifting her chin, she looked out across the waves. She could do this. She could.

In a couple of weeks she'd be right back in the swing of it.

Pleased with her little pep-talk, she looked starboard at the sailboat that had dropped anchor ahead of her.

Shielding her eyes as the evening sun danced on the water, she took in the fine sight.

The sun hit his bare back as he stretched up, checking the rigging.

She'd seen him on the water a few times this summer, and

he'd worked wonders with his boat; she was a real beauty. He certainly hadn't lucked out in the handsome department either.

His arms flexed as he worked, and the muscles in his back moved in response.

Despite his auburn-red hair, his skin had a honeyed tan. The waistband of his cut-offs sat low on his hips, and she found herself swallowing heavily.

Feeling the blush creep into her cheeks, she angled her cap a little lower as she passed.

Glad he hadn't caught her gawking, Ellie rolled her shoulders, trying to shake off her keyed-up mood. The excited barking had her looking back, in time to see a young pup scrabbling across the deck of Mr Handsome's sailboat.

The chewed lead bouncing from his collar told her all she needed to know as he raced for the bow, eyes set on her.

His sooty gaze shone bright with mischief in his shiny black face, as he took a clumsy leap from the deck, falling into the ocean below.

The headsail started to crumple as Handsome turned, clearly his only thought to race for the pup.

Ellie stood, watching in horror as the sail and line fell around him. Time seemed to slow as he lost his balance, struggling to untangle himself. His footing faltered as he shouted for the pup, and tripped, tumbling into the ocean.

"Oh bloody-hell!" Glancing down at the dash, she took a reading on the depth and dropped anchor. Toeing off her deck shoes, she rushed aft and braced her hands on the stern.

The black labrador pup bobbed to the surface, too far away for her to reach him. His laboured strokes and panicked expression had her vaulting over the side.

The chilly water of Langstone Harbour rushed up to meet her, and she let out a gasp as it hit her sun-warmed skin.

Kicking out, she made long, even strokes, swimming for the pup.

Finally managing to loop a finger through his collar, she pulled him to her. His enthusiastic licks peppered her face, as she clutched him against her chest, frantically scanning the water for Handsome.

Continuing to kick, she headed towards his boat, rapidly blinking the salt water from her eyes. She was still trying to clear her vision, when she caught a flash of skin break the surface.

The pup whimpered in her arm, as she swam for his owner. Handsome's movements were sluggish as he rolled over, and the thin trickle of blood at his temple had alarm spiking through her.

His eyes were rolling when she reached him, and planting the pup on his chest, she hooked his collar back through her fingers, using Handsome as a raft. Wrapping her arm under his, she laid on her back, pulling him against her upper body, and kicked out for the boat, thankful it was only a few feet away.

Holding on to the ladder, she wrapped her legs around his waist, anchoring him to her.

Twisting awkwardly, she just about managed to manoeuvre the pup, depositing the shivering creature into the cockpit.

Keeping her legs firmly locked around Handsome's waist, she hooked her arm through a ladder rung, letting them both sway in the calm waters, while she caught her breath.

Slowly turning him to fully face her, she gently eased the heavy fall of hair away from his temple, more than a little relieved to only find a shallow cut. He had a nasty knot, nothing that looked too serious, but she'd get him out of the water and make sure of it.

As the adrenaline that had been pumping through her system slowly calmed down, she lifted slightly astonished eyes to the sky. She was wrapped round a man, hanging off the back of his boat. It most definitely wasn't what she'd thought would be happening this evening.

She stared at his angular features, frowning slightly at the energy she felt pouring from him. Uncertain if she was still buzzed, she laid a hand in the centre of his chest to read his aura, releasing a shocked gasp at the surge of old power thrumming through him.

In his unconscious state he seethed with magics.

He seemed to still beneath her palm, his eyelids fluttering, and as he came to, he must have thrown up metaphysical barriers, as any trace of magic faded away.

Watching his eyes, relieved when they properly focused, she was surprised to find a smile tip his lips.

"Hey, Beautiful." His voice was deep and throaty, and she couldn't help but chuckle.

"Hey yourself. Do you think you can get back on board?" She waited, as he tried to process what had happened.

He looked around, groaning when he touched the bump on his head. "I went overboard. Christ."

His big hand unconsciously wrapped around her thigh, as he tested his legs beneath the water, and heat flooded her face. It was one thing when he'd been knocked out, but now, she literally had a man between her legs!

Trying to hide her mortification, she did her best to stay focused as she agreed with him. "That you did. Now then, do you think you can get up the ladder?"

His piercing blue gaze sent fissions racing through her, as his hand flexed on her thigh. "Well, I've definitely been in worse positions than this. But I suppose I could give it go."

Refusing to be drawn into flirting with a man who'd just knocked himself unconscious, she unfolded her legs from around him, making sure he stayed afloat before leaning away from the ladder. "If you wouldn't mind."

Slowly pulling himself from the water, she tried not to notice tanned skin, tight muscle and delicious thighs. Raising her brows she looked away; she'd really need to work on that.

Cursing her blushing, she bit her lip. Gods, he was gorgeous. And she was crap with men.

Not that anyone she came into contact with was like him. Her uni lectures were full of pranksters and pot-heads.

The slight cough from above had her cringing as she looked up, to find him leaning over the bow with his hand outstretched towards her.

"You coming aboard, or you just gonna stay in the water?"

Reaching up, she clasped his hand, detecting again the faintest whisper of old power. She'd get him sorted, and be on her way.

She was nineteen for crying out loud, she could handle this.

Her feet barely touched the ladder as he wrenched her from the ocean. The strength of him had her mouth going dry, as his hands settled on her shoulders, steadying her.

She could handle this. She could. Dammit.

"Okay?"

Nodding, Ellie took a breath, settling herself, before lifting calmer eyes to his. "I'm good. Thank you. Now, let's get the little one sorted, then I'll have a look at your head."

The pup was still shivering, looking pretty sorry for himself, as Ellie went to her knees in the cockpit.

"I'll grab a towel." As he headed below deck, she could hear him muttering that the dog was like 'bloody Houdini'.

Slowly murmuring to the exhausted fella, she picked him up, running her hands over him.

Centering her energy she let the healing warmth fill her, pooling it in her palms. Stroking over him, his shivers began to lessen, and his pained breathing eased.

The angry swelling in his right shoulder, where he'd hit

the water, faded away, and Ellie released a relieved sigh as she felt him wriggle in her embrace; now he felt better, he wanted to be free.

The second his paws touched the deck he began shaking the water from his fur. Droplets sprayed all around her, leaving her laughing as she stroked his silky ears. "Aren't I wet enough?"

"Come on, Murphy, give her a break." He stood just a few inches away, a towel wrapped round his shoulders; he'd taken the worst of the water from his hair, and held another in his hand. His smile was welcoming, as he held the towel towards her. "He's feeling better then? Here, you could do with this more than the trouble-maker."

Picking up the longer length of frayed makeshift lead, that was still secured to the railing, he looped it back through Murphy's collar, giving the pup a serious look. "We're going to have to work harder on your water safety, my friend."

Soaking up what she could, Ellie watched as he smoothed Murphy's head, the little labrador beamed back up at him. He was clearly adored.

Pulling herself together, Ellie rung out her hair. Her cap was lost to the waves, so she loosely secured the wet, salty mess in a bun.

"He's feeling better now, his shoulder will be fine." She gestured to the low seat. "If you'll sit I can have a look at your head."

Carefully placing his hands around the pup's upper body he smoothed the fur, checking him over before looking up at her.

"I'm Adam, by the way. And it's just a knock, I'll be fine."

Ellie looked into his eyes as he spoke, nothing alarming sat in his aura, but that 'knock' could leave him with a concussion. "I'm sure it will be, but it would put my mind at rest if you'll just let me check."

Coming to his feet he gave her another of those killer smiles as he eased past her, the little cockpit left barely breathing room for the three of them.

Even sat down, the expanse of him was overwhelming. Staring at him she figured he must play rugby, his shoulders were so broad.

Looking down, she hurriedly wiped her hands on the towel. Her attempt at averting her gaze left her staring at his thighs. They too were packed with muscle; solid and strong, and she took a heavy swallow and a deep breath, inwardly rolling her eyes.

Get a grip on yourself, Ellie Thaine!

Stepping towards his spread legs she raised her hand, carefully moving his hair. The sun picked up the gold in the burnished depths. The bump had stopped bleeding, and she breathed evenly, focusing her energy as her Mother had taught her and her brother.

"What was wrong with Murphy's shoulder?"

"Hmmm?" The question reached her slowly, as she worked to pool her power. "Oh, he hit the water awkwardly, but he'll be okay, I gave him an all over boost, so he'll be even more of a handful for a while."

"A boost?" His tone was confused as he spoke, and Ellie felt something niggle her subconscious as she held her hands just above his wound.

The second her charged palms touched his aura she felt his energy crackle around her, and he jerked his head up.

"What's happening?"

Ellie shook her head, her startled eyes meeting his. "I'm not sure, I've never healed someone who carries your kind of old magic before." *Never healed someone who had any kind of magic before...*

The very air around them began to thrum, vibrating with power as Ellie felt a wave of energy pour from the ether, it was like a sigh from the ocean as the tide rolled in; relief seemed to breathe all around them, as if something were clicking into place.

His hands gripped her hips, hard. "What do you mean, *magic?*" His voice was harsh and his eyes were wide as they held her gaze.

"Your magic— not mine, I'm a healer, but you..." A horrible realisation dawned. The knot and the cut on his head had gone, but power coursed through him. Between them.

He hadn't been barriering his magic after all. His magic had been asleep, latent...

He came to his feet in a rush, still holding her. Ellie tried to jerk back, but he was too strong. She must have opened some sort of channel. His magic was taking what it needed from her. Somehow she'd woken it up.

"Adam, let me go!" Her voice was stark, and fear trilled through her as she looked at him. A burning rim of gold now ringed his blue irises. "Your eyes..."

He closed them tightly, shaking his head. "I. Don't. Want. This." His spoke through gritted teeth, and she could finally feel the fight within him as he struggled to pull away from her. "I don't want this!"

The shout left his lips as they wrenched apart, the force sent her staggering back.

The gold had eclipsed the blue, as if fire danced in his eyes. "Adam..." She had no idea what to say, or what to do, slowly taking a step towards him.

Rage and horror lit his gaze as he looked at her. "What have you done?" he clutched his head as he sank back onto the bench.

Taking another step closer she held her hands wide, "I don't know. I thought... The magic was all around you."

His eyes were deadly as he looked up at her. "What have you done?!"

Cutting her off, Thea shook her head. "No really, please let me explain. Please?"

Getting the key in the lock, and pushing the door open, she flipped light switches and turned the thermostat up. Sod it only being September, she was bloody freezing.

Nerves trilled through her as they went into the kitchen. If this was about magic, maybe, finally, she'd have the courage to tell Thea what she'd long suspected.

Leaning back against the kitchen side, Ellie waited while Thea sat down, and the rain began a heavier patter on the glass roof of the conservatory.

"Okay Thea, you've got the floor. Although heavens knows what this is all about."

Taking a deep breath, Thea let out a sigh. "I've been avoiding you." It was a soft rush of words, followed by a sad laugh as she pushed to her feet to pace. "Oh Ellie, I had a whole speech worked out, that would explain all my *reasons*. But that feels foolish now."

Coming to a standstill, Thea set her jaw and looked at Ellie. "I was going to tell you that I was afraid of putting you in the middle; Marc is your brother and when things didn't work out between him and me, I didn't want you to feel pulled. But that's not true, it was just an excuse that I used to try and make it easier to face the fact that I was losing my best friend and Marc."

Taking another breath she walked to the back door, staring out at the rain as it dripped on Ellie's pretty garden.

"When I found out that my ancestor had cursed—or *forced*—your family line to be tied to mine, I thought I would have to give you up... or something like that anyway."

Thea's brown eyes looked beseechingly at Ellie, as if begging her for forgiveness, and Ellie found that she couldn't get the words past the lump in her throat, as her eyes glazed with hot tears that wanted to fall.

"So I've avoided you, I couldn't face you, I've used work and *being busy* as excuses. I'd lashed out at Marc, blaming him for things our ancestors did, and hid from it all." She finished the last with a lift of her chin, as if ready to bear the fallout. "And I'm sorry."

Ellie opened her mouth to speak, but Thea rushed on.

"I know I've been a poor excuse for a friend, wrapped up in my own goings-on, while you're worrying about your brother and probably me too. And even though you wouldn't admit it, you must have your doubts about Adam being in the bay now. I've been so busy trying to stay out of it, and just being pleased that my brother is back that I've not been there for you..."

A teary laugh left Ellie's lips as rushed to hug her friend. Some of the constant churning of the last few weeks finally easing within her.

Finding Thea laughing and having a little cry too made Ellie laugh more fully. "Now you listen to me, you crazy-woman. No *curse,* and no medieval witch could force me to be your friend, my friendship is freely given. And yes, having Adam back in the bay *is* hard." As Thea opened her mouth to ask, Ellie shook her head, stepping back. "And no, I don't want to explain why."

Reaching into the cupboard, she pulled out a box of tissues and put them on the table. "Come and sit with me." Whisking a couple of tissues from the box, she dried her eyes and smiled at her closest friend. The weight of the guilt and the worry shifted within her, but for the first time a sense of peace sat with it. "Adam is your brother, and you should be happy to have him home. And I'm sorry too, because the problems between him and me make you feel like you can't share that with me. And in the same way you don't want me to be in the middle with you and Marc, I've never wanted to go into things about Adam. But..." She took a deep breath, still trying to process how quickly the Universe could just throw life at you. "But I will. Not today, because sorting this," she gestured between them, "between you and me is important. But soon, and I'd like Jess to be here when I do."

At the mention of her sister, Thea's eyes widened. "That serious, huh?"

Slowly nodding, Ellie searched for the right words. "I think so. I think I need to get a few things straight for myself, first. And we haven't spoken properly since you *saw* the past, and I'd like us to talk more about that too. There's so many questions we need answered, and things we need to face, and I think the time for that is fast approaching. You said, back in the summer, that you felt change was coming. So do I. And it's tired of waiting for us to be ready."

"Ellie, you are my best friend, another sister to me." Taking her hand, Thea let out a sigh, offering a watery smile. "I am sorry, so very sorry. We do need to deal with everything, and I've been burying my head in the sand. I should have come to you sooner."

Letting out a weepy chuckle of her own, Ellie dabbed at her eyes, gripping Thea's hand equally as tight. "Will you stop, I love you like my own sister."

As they smiled at each other, a sadness washed through her. "I am sorry you and Marc couldn't work it out, give it time, he—"

"Uh—" Thea's stutter was cut off as high pitched yip sounded from the back garden.

"What the...?" Pushing to her feet, Ellie unlocked the back door, to admit her dripping wet brother. "Marc! What are you doing here? You're soaking!"

His grin was broad from beneath his massive raincoat, as he all but filled the tiny kitchen, wrapping his sister in a damp hug.

The yip sounded again, louder this time. Ellie stepped

back, totally confused at the sight of a little yellow puppy, pushing her face above the zipper, her tongue lolling and her canine smile wide.

"I waited for ages before coming over, but after hanging about in the back garden I figured if you two were just going to sit there weeping all night, I may as well come in.."

"Marc..." Ellie shook her head, and looked to Thea, unsure of what on earth was happening.

But Thea had already rushed to her feet, tugging on Marc's coat zipper to release the excited ball of fur. "Oh Poppy, are you stuck in there." Scooping the pup up to her chest, Thea lifted her lips for a kiss, and smiled as Marc obliged.

Lightly patting his chest, she stepped back. "And we weren't going to *weep all night.*" Before turning to face Ellie. "This was the other thing I wanted to tell you." Giving Marc a long look, she shook her head. "If I'd had time..."

Hanging his coat on the hook, Marc dropped his arm across Thea's shoulders, before lightly stroking the puppy. His hair had grown out from the brutally short military cut he'd had eight weeks ago, and he was grinning like a lottery winner.

But as Ellie looked at the picture the three of them made together, she supposed he had every right. "You, uh, sorted it out then?"

Stepping towards her, Thea lifted her questioning gaze, her voice soft. "We did. Yesterday. I... I was going to go to Yorkshire and tell him I'd been an idiot. But he came back before I could."

"Brought the pup with me too, figured that'd sweeten my chances."

Trying to sift through everything she was being told, Ellie touched her brow. "The puppy's yours..."

"Sure, and you're going to be Auntie Ellie."

16

Sending Marc an exasperated look, Thea hushed him. "Will you just hold on a minute. Ellie, is this okay? All this?" Thea's swept her hand in a circle, encompassing them all.

Looking at the happiness on their faces, Ellie could only smile. "You guys, you... I'm so bloody happy for you. But how? Marc what about your work? Thea are you leaving?" Taking a breath she plopped down in the chair, holding up her hands with a laugh. "Questions don't matter. You'll manage."

Giving his sister what could only be described as a sloppy smile, he took her hand, pulling her to her feet, his voice soft when he spoke. "Of course we will, we'll all manage, together. Ells, I'm coming home."

Wrapping him in a bear hug, she laughed and cried, pulling Thea in too. Tonight's paperwork would have to wait.

CHAPTER 1

OCTOBER (2017)

THE LOW VIBRATION in his pocket had him reaching for his phone.

Adam stared down at the screen: no caller ID.

"Hello?"

"Well now, and isn't that a voice to bring a smile to my face."

The rhythmic Irish brogue dropped through him like a dead weight.

"Dillon." Adam didn't bother asking how he'd got this number, or what he wanted.

He'd known Dillon would turn up eventually. He'd just hoped that eventually would turn into a few decades.

"Adam. So you're back in the bay, and been there for a while, I gather. You know, I didn't figure you for the homebody type."

The veiled malice crawled across him, leaving an almost tangible layer of grime on his skin.

"We all change. What do you want?" He deliberately kept his voice even and calm. He could

feel Dillon tapping at the edges of his energetic field, seeing if there were any cracks in his armour, if there was any way in.

He was careful to keep his rage banked, not wanting to give Dillon anything to draw out, anything to latch on to.

"Want? Why, I don't want anything, boyo." Wretched glee dripped from each word. "But you see, I'm in London. Doing a bit of a protection favour for a friend, so I am. You see, his normal witch was busy, she'd had to fly off. To Greece of all places. Now he's got a real problem, this friend of mine, needed his mojo all topped up. And there I am, doing my thing, and imagine my surprise when I pick up the distinct traces of Lavelle magic. Naturally I'd recognise it."

Adam's grip on the phone tightened with each word, the tension across his shoulders pooling, burning a red-hot trail down his spine. He gritted his teeth against the pain, giving Murphy a fierce look. Warning him to stay where he was, he opened the patio door, and stepped out.

Leaving Murphy safely shut inside the house, he headed for the steps that lead down to the ocean. He gritted his teeth against the frustration caused by the leg brace, but he had no choice but to drag himself to the sea. He knew the banked rage and anger was going to come pouring out, nothing could stop it.

The bitterly cold night brought no relief to his searing skin, from the heat bubbling up from the core of him.

"And you know, boyo, it occurred to me; I surely hope that my friend's problem doesn't come looking for your sister."

The line went dead, and Adam dropped the phone to the pebbles. He was powerless, he couldn't even walk properly!

Yanking his hoodie over his head, he hobbled towards the frigid ocean.

The skin on his hips and across the base of his spine tore and stretched as he pushed the cargo shorts away, molten lava bled from within him, ignited by rage, and he couldn't help but yell out as a salty wave hit him. Hissing as it made contact.

The sound was lost to the water as he plunged into its depths. He gave his agonised shouts to the swirling sea, letting the icy depths cool the torturous burning.

Flames licked through his veins, illuminating the water as he swam deeper. Knowing the sea was the only thing that could stop the uncontrollable fire consuming him.

Dillon shut down the mobile, dropping it on the covers. He let his tired body ease down to the plushly-made bed.

Sitting, he stared into the long mirror in front of him. The overtly lavish hotel room fanned out in the reflection. His bare feet were cushioned in the deep carpet, the wall of windows opposite looked out over London. The lights from the London Eye reflected up, from the water of the Thames.

He couldn't afford the hotel suite, but as he stared at himself in the mirror, he watched a small smile lift the edges of his mouth.

"Whether I can afford it or not, don't matter now."

His Irish lineage was obvious, thick red hair, blue eyes, pale skin. His time in Dublin had tainted his southern Irish roots, but he was what he had always been; a witch of the old country.

"And for once, I'd better not let my kin down."

After fifty-three hours of no sleep, his body had become nothing more than one moaning ache, but ignoring the call of the big bed, he pushed to his feet.

Sitting down at the dresser, he slid the mahogany leather desk blotter in front of him. Squaring it up, he placed the pen to the right side, and laid the envelopes above. It was pleasing to him, and he may as well enjoy things that pleased him.

The thick hotel stationary felt good and right beneath his hand, and the smooth noise of the round-nibbed fountain pen calmed his thoughts as he began to write.

He made sure to say sorry for being a royal pain the arse, made sure to ask her to take white tulips to their mother's grave on her birthday, made sure to explain what he'd done.

Laying the pen down, he straightened up, arching the kinks from his spine. He shuffled the two pages together, folding them neatly.

He scrunched his nose at the sharp taste of the seal on the envelope. He'd been five, sat next to his mother on the grass, and she'd helped him write a letter to his grandparents, shown him how to mark a kiss, write the address, where to put the stamp.

He let the bittersweet memory wash over him.

Making the call to room service he requested they come and take the letter.

Holding his hand above it, his low whisper filled the room, his hand shook as magic hazed and the protection spell was complete, and he gloried in the feeling of power. The same as he always had.

The knock on the door had him lifting his head, once-again catching his gaze in the mirror.

"Well, boyo, here we go."

Placing his hand on the crystal doorknob, he felt the power tremor beneath his palms. Once he opened the door the seal would be broken.

"And now's as good a time as any."

Pulling it open, he gave the bellhop a warm Irish smile. "Why thank you, laddie. This letter is for my sister." Placing the letter and a twenty pound note on the tray, he made sure to look the young man straight in the eye. "I want you to see to it, that this gets in the post straightway."

With the courteous response still hanging in the air, Dillon shut the door. As the latch clicked shut a different kind of energy filled the suite.

The long heavy voiles on the windows moved as if caught in a breeze, and the lights flickered and sparked.

Never one to shy away from anything, he drew the curtains as far open as he could, letting in all of the London skyline, before sliding open the large bi-fold doors, welcoming the rainy night.

The sound of the street rose up from below, and he fought a moment of sadness; he loved life. Loved every nuanced moment, but it was fair to say that he'd lived it in a fit of revelry. And he'd be damned if he didn't go out the same way.

"It's no good *hanging* about out there, I let my own protection spell down, so you may as well come in."

Crossing his arms over his chest, he made sure to notice the feel of the fine silk shirt against skin. If he was going out, then by-the-Goddess he was doing it in style.

The tall elegant blonde traced before his eyes, taking form in front of him. Gods', she was lovely.

"You know, it has me wondering, how anything as beautifully packaged as you are, could be so bloody evil."

Her laugh was lilting as she stepped over the threshold. The lights caught the thick, gold slave bangles that wrapped around her upper arms, and her skin had a warm beachy hue, that made her look hot to the touch.

But he knew better.

"Evil is just a word, Cherie. A word created by man, to make other men afraid of a non-existent god." She walked around the suite, touching the fabrics and furniture, stroking the bed. "But then, you also consider yourself evil, do you not?"

Her French accent brought a strange beauty to her words, and the smile he gave her was laced with genuine humour. "Aye, I used to think so. If only I'd met you sooner, I could've put all that behind me. But that's living for you. It is what it is."

As she stopped before him, he found he was pleased, masochistically speaking, to find that his last moments were going to be denying the wants of this truly spectacular creature.

"So, mon Cher, I need the barriers on the museum dropped, and I'd rather you just do it... Than me have to drain every last drop from you, take your memories as my own, and hunt down everyone you know and love." She waved her hand as she spoke, batting away the open threat she'd made.

He smiled into dead eyes, their depths hollow, and waited silently as she studied him, a slight lift to her perfectly shaped lips revealing the deadly tips of her fangs.

"Cherie, I find that you are so much more than I was expecting, maybe you'd prefer I work it out of you another way, non? But you should know, I like to keep my pets." She paused a beat before adding. "So, Dillon O'Leary, of the Clan O'Leary, a hereditary Witch of the Morrigan, what's it going to be?"

Her heated look was enough to convince him that partaking in parlour games with a vampire wasn't for him, and he knew, with certainty, that he'd take death over ever being her play thing.

"*Everyone you know and love*, huh? I'd like to say I don't believe you can do that, but sadly, I know better. And I've wondered for a while if that's how your scourge was slowly creeping back." Deadly rage crawled across her face at his insult, but he merely continued to speak. He'd made his peace, this was where he made his stand. "So here's the deal.

I'll drop the barriers. But only for five of you. In the spirit of fairness and all that."

Her smile had a confused edge as she stared at him, the lengthening of viscous fangs looked erotically right against her lush, red lips.

He said nothing else as she continued to hold him with her gaze, until all pretence of patience was lost.

With a hiss she whirled away, clicking her fingers as she did so.

The chill at his back told him she'd called for another, and in the milliseconds before he could react a smooth feminine hand slid across his throat, to hold his jaw.

Sharp talons dug into his skin, as even sharper teeth scraped his neck.

The blonde was back, standing before him, as the vampire behind him held him pressed against her freezing body. "I was trying to be reasonable."

Struggling to laugh against the grip at his throat, he rolled his eyes heavenward, before rasping. "Reasonable? I don't think so. Tell me, have you actually got close to the Chalice yet? Or does the wolf make you nervous?"

Her warm brown gaze flooded with red as she lashed out. Her claws rent the silk shirt, and his chest beneath it, and he couldn't stifle the groan of agony.

"Bleed him!"

At her command, fangs pierced his skin. The cold was burning.

A chill crawled through his veins, replacing the warmth of his blood.

She stepped against him, pressing fully into the length of him, slipping her fingers into his hair. "I now own every spell you're working. I know everyone you knew, I know *you*. As if you never existed."

The groan from behind him, told him the deal he'd made was working.

The brunette vampire pushed away, throwing him, stumbling.

He hit the floor, cracking his head. He blinked rapidly.

Her long dark hair, and swirling red eyes came back into focus as she pounced over him, pinning him to the floor. Her claws piercing his skin.

"Make it stop! Make it stop!" Her crazy screams reverberated through his brain, the blood loss and poison leaving him dizzy.

A sharp backhand from the blonde knocked her out of the way, sending her smashing into the opposite wall. The picture and frame crashing to the floor, along with the still rabid vampire.

Yanking him up from the floor, her claws digging in, she seethed.. "What have you done?"

The cold had seeped to his very core. Opening his mouth to speak, he found he couldn't form the words, paralysis leaching into every muscle. The final act of a predator he supposed; to render their prey helpless.

She leant closer, as he tried again, the roiling malevolence in her eyes promising vile retribution if she was displeased.

Grinning drunkenly at her, he relished the thought of it. "I told you, that was the deal."

Dropping him unceremoniously to the floor, she spun to her counterpart. "What's happening?"

"There's nothing! He's empty!" She clutched her head. "Only the museum, only nothing, my head..."

Clearly furious, the blonde scored her skin with her claws, letting the blood run freely. Brushing the dark hair away from the face of her companion, she offered her wrist.

With each draw, the smaller vampire seemed to calm,

until finally stepping away with a grateful bow. "Thank you, my Lady."

Dillon slitted his eyes, fighting losing consciousness. He'd wanted to take at least one of them with him, but it wasn't to be. They wouldn't get his memories, or his spells, and he'd called in the cavalry. That would have to be enough.

He longed to hear the chant of distant voices, calling him home. A lone tear escaped, his breath stilling in his lungs. But that would never be.

～

ELLIE YANKED THE STEERING WHEEL, sending her little Mini in a half circle, pebbles spraying across the seafront.

Bolting from the car she ran the length of the beach, stones crunching beneath her soles.

The icy night air stung her face and hurt her lungs as she pumped her arms, running as fast as she could towards Adam's house.

Something was very wrong.

She'd been driving home, barely thinking anything when it had dropped through her; complete, consuming, raw panic. She'd only been halfway across the bridge, leaving the Island, but her pounding heart had her turning the car and racing back.

Adam.

He was hurt.

The sick weight of fear had filled her as she'd sped towards his house.

Ahead of her, his turn of the century house in darkness.

She gasped at the icy night air hitting her cheeks. But with no time to think about a coat she hurried around the back of his house.

Nothing.

Her ballet flats struggled to find purchase as she went down to the beach.

Dread gnawed at her, and she released a moan of relief as she caught sight of his silhouette, standing tall, facing out to sea. He was alone, and he was okay; there was still time to reach him.

Digging in, she fought the freezing air burning her lungs, and ran to get to him.

He was throwing something to the ground, before pulling the sweater over his head.

Her hands flew to cover her cry as she stumbled, going to her knees on the stones.

Her wrenching breaths were all she could hear as she watched in horror.

He took an awkward step towards the ocean, the full boot encasing his healing-leg hampering him.

What looked like red-hot embers lit him from within, tracing the length of his spine to seer the skin of his lower back.

Finally naked he pitched forward into the ocean, his yell triggering a whimper from her as she struggled to her feet, staggering towards him.

The sea hissed and heat hazed as he dropped beneath the surface, water bubbling up around him, glowing red and gold.

Her brain had switched into absolute panic mode. Unable to piece together what was happening, she didn't feel the chill of the ocean or the heat of the steam as she waded in after him. Her only thought: his safety.

She was up to her waist, with the seabed slipping away. The waves splashing against her as she frantically reached into the murky depths.

The burning glow was fading, leaving only the dark ocean and even darker night. The cloud hid any hint of the waxing gibbous, Hunter Moon, and her body had begun to shake in reaction with chill and shock.

As she turned full circle she could hear someone calling his name, and it took precious moments for her to realise it was her. Whispering a litany as she searched for him.

The churning waves calmed around her, as if the seething fury had dispersed from the night air.

He broke the surface, like a demigod born of Poseidon. His auburn hair was longer and thicker than she remembered, and it was plastered around his face, revealing the now golden hue of his once-blue eyes.

He was broad and powerful; could've been carved from marble.

His hands fisted and unfurled as he drew in great heaving breaths, that were visible in the icy night. Before finally closing his eyes, lifting his face to the night sky, letting the newly falling rain soothe him.

"Adam..." His name left her lips once more, as she took a step towards him. Reaching out she was stunned to see the light blue glow of her palms, her need to heal him, to help him, so unbearably intense. "Let me——"

He turned, the move slow and measured. His golden gaze fastened on her. He seemed to be taking her in, studying every inch of her as they booth swayed with the rhythm of the bitter sea.

"Let you... Let you what?"

The short staccato of his words hit like bullets, and she dropped her arms to her sides, self-consciously hiding her hands, letting them hang beneath the surface of the water.

Unable to form words, she shook her head. Not knowing where to begin. Not understanding any of this.

His arms lifted as he spoke, gesturing at his body. "Haven't you done enough to my family—to me?"

Years ago the poisoned hatred of his words would have

sent her running. They *had*. She'd holed up to lick her wounds, trying to work through the guilt, trying to make any of it make sense.

But it wasn't years ago, and she'd spent the years since coming to accept that she hadn't done anything wrong. It was far-beyond time that she got to have her say.

Pure, unadulterated anger poured through her as she looked at him.

The clouds had begun to move, letting through slices of the moon's light.

Burns and scars littered his hips, curling around them. But as the ocean lapped at him, each wave healed, until finally only smooth, tanned skin remained.

Planting her hands on her hips, she took a deep, shivering, breath.

Finally.

Finally she was going to have her say.

"What *I've* done? This isn't me, you fool. This is *you*. This is what lives in you." Her voice rose, "I didn't put the magic there. It already existed! Nothing was going to stop that level of power from finding a way out."

She threw her hands wide, shouting out him. "Don't you get it? It was *time!* Even if it hadn't been me, it would still have happened." Her palm hit the water with a slap, her temper flowing full and fierce, in a way she never allowed. She'd put up with his cold ignorance for years, stayed away from her friends; his sister, when he came home. She'd let his deathly apathy push her out. She'd hidden like a scared doe.

Well, no more. No, bloody, more.

"I am so sick of your shit." Her voice rose as the clouds rolled completely away, the pale bands of moonlight laying across them. "You blame me, because that's easy for you, so that you don't have to look any further than me; so you don't have to look at *you*. Well there's so much more to this than you know, and I am so bloody tired of being your whipping boy."

The flat-eyed look she was so used to seeing settled across his face, and she knew he hadn't heard her. But it didn't matter. He might not understand that she'd crossed a line. But she did; there was no going back.

His voice held a vicious edge as his words reached her. "Well, haven't you grown up. The last time you stuck your nose in where it didn't belong and met my temper you ran away."

Throwing back her shoulders, she lifted her chin, ignoring how the water was numbing her legs and making her bottom lip tremble. "Well, not anymore. My life is here, in the bay—on the Island, and if you're back for good, then you'd better get used to seeing a lot of me. Your sisters and my brother are everything to me, and you won't push me out. I won't let you."

Despite the angry set of his jaw, he seemed to be muttering beneath his breath. Fiery magic hazed in his palms, and with one final glare in her direction, he said, "Then you'd better get used to me, because I'm not going anywhere either."

The waves jerked around him as little flashes of gold sparked the night air, and he disappeared. Leaving wisps of smoke in his wake.

The flash of movement out of the corner of her eye, had her looking up at his house, to see him standing inside—in the warm. The moon bathed the unfairly glorious, naked length of him for a minute, before he turned away.

Her shoulders dropped, any last vestige of energy draining out of her, as freezing shivers wracked her whole body. Shouting at a naked, angry witch, while stood waist deep in the ocean in October, must've been among the top three stupidest things she'd done in this life.

Slowly dragging her freezing body towards the shore, Ellie wrapped her arms around herself, rubbing her chilled skin. She may be a healer who drew strength from the sea, but she could still end up with bloody hypothermia.

As she made the last few steps from the shallows, teeth chattering and body shivering, she held her hands before her, closing her eyes and placing her palms together.

She drew intense healing warmth from her core, willing the energy down through her legs and up into her arms.

The shivers began to subside, and as she opened her eyes she looked down. No light emanated from her palms. Her healing worked, but with no outside signs, just as it usually did.

The night air picked at her wet clothes, as she trudged the length of the beach, back to her car, still leaving her shivering.

As she looked at her hands, her thoughts wandered to Thea. They had been best friends since Uni, and it'd been over a year before Ellie had worked out that Adam was her brother.

She turned her hands over as she walked, looking at them. She'd never had visible signs of her power, her healing ability had always been something that she had *felt*.

The only times her palms lit-up was when she was with Thea or her sister Jess. And now Adam.

There were so many questions about the connection between their families.

Reaching her Mini, she eased her wet self into the driver's seat, catching her reflection in the review mirror. Her blue eyes stared back at her, and she gave herself a firm nod. "It's time to get some answers."

As soon as Thea and Marc got back from visiting her and Marc's parents in Yorkshire, she'd tell them. Tell them every-thing; how she'd met Adam, and how all their magic was probably awake because of her. And maybe they could start to figure this thing out.

Adam...

After all these years he still stunned her. Put him within a couple of miles and she felt his pain, she felt *him*. It left her restless and confused. And as ever, drawn to him.

Ellie knew that both Thea and Jess thought Adam shunned all magic from his life. But considering how he'd shifted his form from the ocean to his living room, and the firework display she'd just witnessed, it was clear he was hiding things from all of them. Stopping outside her cottage she turned the engine off, still trying to calm her charged nerves.

They were never going to be able to figure out what the hell all this was about unless everyone was honest, and she very much doubted he'd be inclined to share with her.

Her short mutter lifted to the rolling clouds as she unlocked her front door.

"Well tough."

CHAPTER 2

HIS WHOLE BODY thrummed with magic, as he reformed in the living room. It trilled through his system, so pure and bright.

Perfect.

He'd never been able to get the balance; it was either all magic or all rage. No in-between.

Adam turned back to the beach, looking through the patio doors; she still stood in the ocean, shivering.

Turning, she looked up at him, her expression unreadable. Her sky-blue eyes flicked down the length of him, and he damned the lust that pooled low in his gut. Deliberately keeping his look one of annoyed boredom, he turned away into the shadows to watch her unseen.

The waves pulled at her as she took faltering steps towards the shore, her dark hair was longer than it had been all those years ago. It hung down her back, the breeze lifting it. And as always when it came to Ellie, he had to fight the urge to go to her. To warm her chilled skin, to take her in his arms.

She was petit and dainty compared to him,, and he'd dreamed many times over the years of having her in his embrace.

The moon bathed her as she stood on the shore, hands clasped together in front of her, head slightly bent. Invisible energy buzzed around her, and her skin lost the blue tinge the icy ocean had given her.

Her closed eyes softened with relief; she was warming herself, and he found the act of watching her skin turn pink incredibly erotic.

Ignoring the obvious effect she always had on his body, he turned away and met Murphy's frustrated gaze.

"I know, you think I'm a jerk. Gimme a break, Murph."

The disgruntled labrador merely held his gaze, silently agreeing with Adam's words, until he raised his hands, palms up. "There's just all this, I don't know— *stuff* between us. And I *know;* you like her. You chased her into the ocean for gods' sakes."

Raising knowing brows at him, Murphy waited, tilting his head.

"It's always been easier to be angry at her. At least that way, she just gave me a wide berth." Shaking his head, he released a heavy sigh. Bending down, he rubbed Murphy's soft ears. "But, old friend,

it seems like those days are over. I'd just hoped I'd have all three bottles before I went to Thea and Jess.

And now this with Dillon..." His voice trailed away as he straightened up.

Now wasn't the time to overthink, now he had to get hold of Jess, and make sure that the type of trouble that followed Dillon O'Leary around stayed far away from her.

Picking up his mobile phone from the kitchen side, he rolled his shoulders, clearing his mind and his aura.

He'd long ago cast a spell that barriered his sisters from knowing when he was 'up a creek without a paddle'. But he had to be a lot more careful when he was with them, or talking to them. The last thing he needed was to involve them in this mess.

Dialling Jess, he stared out at the night sky; the moon would be full tomorrow night. Staring at its brightness as the clouds cleared, he couldn't shake the worry gnawing at him with each ring.

As it clicked over to answer phone, he closed his eyes, throwing out a diaphanous web, searching for her.

Coming up empty, he frowned at Murphy, before trying again, this time looking for Thea.

Her light energy filled him, making him smile. He pinned her down to the north, and she was happy, laughing. He also detected distinctly good food. Which he knew would make her even happier.

Letting her go, he tried again for Jess, unable to find even a hint of her energetic field.

"Where the bloody hell is she?"

Murphy was fully alert, his stance solid and strong as he waited.

Taking a breath, he calmed his thoughts, needing to keep them clear. Rage made his mind foggy, and now, more than ever, he needed control.

Looking at the stairs, he groaned at the heavy weight of the walking boot encasing his left leg. Gods' dammit, everything took so much longer with this blessed-bloody leg still healing.

Cursing under his breath he struggled with the stairs, until his bedroom came into view, and he was able to focus his energy and haze inside.

Looking at the array of magical items across his dresser, he chose a hand-sized amethyst geode. Turning it in his palms, he lifted it to the window, letting the moon's light catch each little point.

Standing in the window, he scanned the length of the beach below, making sure no-one was about. Staring at the shore line, he pictured himself there, feeling the crackling energy pour through him, heating his nerve endings.

He let the sensation of fracturing apart wash over him, until he reformed at the edge of water.

Plunging his empty hand up to the elbow in the salty sea, he cast his gaze back to Murphy, sat in the living room, watching him, and once again hazed back into his home.

Making his way to the fireplace, he opened the door to the unlit log burner, rubbing the crystal and his wet hand through the soot.

The powdery blackness coated his fingers.

He traced a triskelion on the centre of his chest, before drawing magic to his palms, and pulled soot from the fireplace.

The gold, sizzling energy of his power, lifted each particle across the room, laying an identical triskelion on the hardwood living room floor.

Elevating the amethyst geode from his grasp, he levitated it above the sigil.

Voices of old trickled with the moon's rays, brushing across his bare skin, as the heavy weight of ancient magic rent the air, and he whispered his spell into the night.

> Hear me spirits,
> I search for one I hold dear.
> Her magic is electric,
> Her blood-line Lavelle.
> I sense danger around her,
> Show her to me now.

The scent of rain crept into the air, as the geode began to tremor. Images raced behind his closed eyes, like pieces of dreams; fragmented and broken. Jess...

She stood at her window, here in the bay, staring out at the rain. Then the train, all the colours and noise. The underground and the Thames, warm coffee and laughter, takeaway food and the museum...

The museum came again and again, like a stuck record, whipping around him. From day into night. He could see the warm lights, marble busts, the large doors to the gallery of the Victoria and Albert.

Magic vibrated, pushing against him as it fought to find her. Until finally, it knocked him off his feet — she was on a floor, her long dark hair wild, eyes glowing lavender, while her magic raged around her. She threw up her palms, hiding herself from all; from him.

As the image faded, he wrenched in heaving breaths, the fevered red eyes of a female vampire filling his vision.

Pushing to his feet with a shout, he staggered across the living room as the geode dropped to the floor. A chill wind tore through the room, tearing the triskelion from the floor and his skin, whirling the black soot up and throwing it back into the fireplace, where it crackled and hissed, disappearing into the ether.

Leaning heavily against the back of the sofa, he tried to calm his erratic breathing. Cold sweat coated him, and his thoughts were scattered. But fire licked beneath his skin, curling to the surface.

She was in trouble.

The rage and helplessness flashed hard and quick within him, and he clenched his fists against the searing heat.

Murphy's short, sharp bark had him looking at his friend. As always, the stoic stare stopped him in his tracks.

"Alright Murphy." He struggled to form the words, but

caught sight of the moon shining on the inky ocean. He watched each wave, as it rose and broke, fighting for the control that tried to constantly evade him. "I'm reigning it in." Another breath, another wave. "I'm getting there."

Each step to the kitchen was hampered by the leg brace, but he focused on his phone.

Flicking through the contacts he hit dial.

"Good evening, The Royal Oak."

"Steve, it's Adam."

"Hey there, I heard you were still in the bay. Why haven't you been in for a pint?"

The cheerful voice of one of his oldest friends helped to bring control that little bit closer. "I'm sure Thea told you I broke my leg, and lord-knows, I could do without the jibes from you. Mate, I know it's short notice, but can Murphy come and keep your Max company for a few days? Jess needs some last minute help at the museum, before some exhibition opens tomorrow, and you know how Murph hates the city."

"Sure thing, you bringing him now, or do you need me to come get you?"

Quickly grasping for an excuse, Adam cleared his throat. He didn't want anyone here right now. He wasn't risking anything. "Nah, don't worry, it's nearly last orders, you stay there. Murph and I'll be over in a bit."

Hanging up the phone, he looked to Murphy. "Well, old friend. It looks like you're going to experience *hazing* tonight. 'Cos I can't get us to the pub any other way."

At Murphy's sombre expression, Adam stroked his ear, rubbing his chin. "Buddy, I can't take you, I don't know what I'm going to find. I need you where I know you're safe. I can only worry about one of you at a time, okay?"

Giving him an understanding look, Murphy pawed his hand, before coming to his feet.

"Okay then, let's get moving."

Murphy sat next to Max outside the pub, the two of them already eyeing the water and deciding whether they should make a run for it, as Adam took good-natured ribbing from his friend.

"Murph'll be fine. Say hi to Jess."

"Will do, and have Lisa save a decent sized piece of steak for me."

At the mention of his pretty wife who ran the kitchen, Steve grinned. "Sure thing. Take it easy."

Slowly turning away, Adam gave Murphy a final nod as he headed up the High Street of the one-road village. He could see Ellie's front door, but couldn't risk hazing in amongst all these windows. The thump-step of his gait really did make him sound like the pirate Steve had just compared him to.

Checking his watch, he could see pinpricks of light in her upstairs window, but the rest of the house was in darkness.

11.10pm. "It's not that bloody late." His low mutter was accompanied by the ringing of her doorbell as he leant on it.

The sudden activity from within had him standing straight. The hallway light clicked on, and he could see her blurry image rushing down the stairs.

Wrenching the front door open, worried blue eyes stared into his. "What's wrong?"

It figured that she'd have picked up on something.

Stepping over the threshold he pushed the door shut behind. "I need you to drive me to London. Now."

He'd hadn't thought about what he'd expected her to do. But the total loss of expression from her face, the slow raise of her brows and a concise "No," wasn't it.

The sense of urgency running through him hit a wall as he stared at her. Panic teasing at the edges of his mind, as, not for the first time in recent weeks, he was reminded anew that he couldn't rely solely on himself at the moment. He needed others. And to keep his sister safe he needed someone he knew he could trust.

Knowing that he could trust her grated on his nerves, as did knowing that she wasn't going to help him in any way without an explanation. "Look—"

Shaking her head quickly, her shiny hair shimmered around her face, the hallway light picking up the flecks of honey in the chocolate depths.. Adam set his jaw, loathing himself for noticing.

Crossing her arms firmly she cleared her throat, he also noticed her soft-looking chequered pyjamas, and cursed himself.

"No, you look. If you think I'm going to be your lackey now that your sisters aren't running around after you, you need to grow a brain." Briefly looking down, and behind him, a frown settled on her brow as she stepped back. "And where's Murphy?"

Maintaining his calm, he clenched and unclenched his hands in the pockets of his cargo shorts. Rubbing his thumb over the smooth slice of howlite that was supposed to help.

Nothing bloody helps.

"Murphy's at the pub." Looking down at her, he realised they'd barely said more than a dozen words to each other in seven years. "I've left him there, because Jess is in trouble, and I need your... help." The final word stuck in his throat, and he figured she probably thought he hated having to ask *her*. In truth, he hated having to ask anyone.

She tilted her head as she looked at him, expression wary, her arms falling to her hips. "What kind of trouble?"

Unable to keep banking down the panic, which would undoubtedly set off his temper, he deliberately kept every word succinct. Focusing on nothing but forming the sentence. "Ellie, 'please' isn't something I say easily. And I will explain, but can we *please* just get going?" He knew from the fissions bouncing about inside him that his eyes must be changing, and the flashes of heat hitting his nerve endings were a sure sign that he was losing the battle of control.

He opened his mouth, unsure what else he could say to make her understand, when she gave him a decisive nod.

Turning from him, racing up the stairs, she flung a "Wait there," over her shoulder, as her bedroom door slammed behind her.

Within minutes, dressed in jeans and a black roll neck, she was back, snug red trainers encasing her feet. She darted down the hallway, opening the under-the-stairs cupboard, and pulling out a beaten-up looking leather satchel.

"Let's go."

Putting the satchel in the boot of her little Mini Clubman, she hurried to the passenger side, holding the door as wide as she could, so he could try to drop down easier into the bucket seats.

"What kind of a car is this anyway?" Adam's gruff moaning grated on her nerves, as she slammed the door shut.

"A car that's going to get you where you need to go..." Releasing her response though gritted teeth, where no-one but the night sky could hear her, she took a calming breath of her own as she walked round the car. The chill October air stung, and her warm exhale plumed in the icy night.

She was about to voluntarily shut herself in a small space with Adam Lavelle. If it wasn't for Jess...

Shutting the door, she clicked her belt into place and started the ignition.

The road out of the bay was silent and still, and the clouds had cleared to reveal the stars of Orion's Arm.

More cars joined them as she took the north route, hitting the A3 to London.

"Tell me what's going on, Adam." He'd seemed to calm the minute they'd started moving, the waves of energy that had been pouring from him in her hallway easing with each mile they covered.

But he still crackled sat next to her, all down her left side seemed to fizz at his close proximity. And in her little car that meant *close*, his six foot plus frame was so much larger when confined. His head virtually brushed the ceiling, and he had adjusted the seat fully back, until it was touching the seat behind.

"What's in the bag?" He shifted awkwardly, sitting side on, to look at her.

Sparing him a quick glance, the orangey-gold still ringed his blue eyes, and she had to ignore the quick jolt that hit her system at just being this close to him, his scent wrapping around her.

It had been years, and he hated her. And still she yearned for him. Silently cursing her own stupidity, she checked the motorway, pulling into the fast lane, before answering him.

"A conversation doesn't work if all both parties do is ask questions. And me helping you won't happen, unless I get some answers." Straightening her posture at the wheel, she lifted her chin, proud of her even tone and calm response. "But in the efforts of good will, I keep the satchel packed with anything that might be useful for a healing. Including first aid supplies. Now, what's going on?"

He was totally still beside her, as if clamping down on all aspects of himself, keeping everything in check.

She'd expect him to be tense in the face of either of his sisters being in trouble. But after what she'd witnessed earlier this evening, it was clear he was struggling to control—or even understand—his magic or himself.

"Okay." Relaxing slightly, he leaned back into the seat,

seeming to search for the words. "Jess isn't answering her phone."

Ellie waited a few beats before huffing a breath, knowing her voice had risen, but unable to curb the annoyance in her tone, she glared at him. "And? Jesus, Adam, get to the bloody point."

She could see the muscle in his jaw tick, but her frayed nerves didn't give a hoot about his temper at this point. "I mean it, you need to start talking, or I'm turning around."

"A... *friend* called me. Earlier this evening, that's why I was —you know—when you found me." He'd clasped his hands loosely on his lap, seeming to concentrate fully on each inhale and exhale, while staring sightlessly ahead. "He said there'd been some activity at the museum; the V & A, and that Jess's protection spells for the building had been interfered with, leaving it open to... other, well, I don't what you know, or—"

Rolling her eyes Ellie cut him off, "I'm well aware there are more witches and people of power out there, if that's what you mean. Surely you didn't think the three of you were the only ones. Arrogant much?" Knowing she was deliberately baiting him, but unable to stop herself, she raised a brow as she looked over at him. Purposely loading the stare with disdain. "Gimme a break."

Inwardly pleased with herself, she watched from the corner of her eye as he tried to shift in the seat, frowning and glaring at everything from the car, to the road, to her.

"Of course I know there's more than us!" His voice boomed in the confines of the Mini. "I just didn't know what you knew, and it can be a shock to some people. I was trying to be thoughtful!" He all but shouted the last word, as if he was doing her a favour.

"You? I've never heard such tripe." Gripping the wheel she checked the rear-view mirror, the coastline behind them had long disappeared from view, and as always, in times of stress she preferred even a glimpse of ocean; it was going to be a long... whatever this turned out to be. "Let's just cut the chat, and get there. Unless there is anything significant or helpful you'd like to share?"

She could see the silhouette of his profile in her peripheral vision, as he silently stared at the road. He clearly wasn't going to answer, and it unnerved her. It shouldn't, she knew she should be used to it. But the Fates clearly had quite a sense of humour, throwing them together, or maybe she was a glutton for punishment? You'd think after all these years she'd have settled in to a cool dislike of him. But no, just the sight of him still made her stomach clench.

It just wasn't fair.

It didn't help that she'd seen him at his best; laughing and joking with Thea and Jess, how much he cared for Murphy. He had friends all over the bay, and was welcomed with open arms whenever he came home.

It really was only her that he shunned. And even though she'd come to understand, and know to be true, the words she'd all but screamed at him on the beach, she still carried the weight of the guilt, that she'd been the one to wake the magic that he clearly didn't want.

There was an undeniable chemistry between them, that couldn't be one-sided, and she wondered, not for the first time, how different things would've been if it hadn't been time for his magic to spark to life.

Frowning as she drove, she flicked her gaze over to him. "And another thing, why am I driving you to London? Why didn't you just teleport? And assuming that's how you got to me, you should be more careful. In the last eight hours I've seen you use tremendous displays of power, and if I've seen it, so can others."

"'Teleport.'" Snorting at her description he looked at her, his expression rife with sarcasm. "It's called *hazing.*"

The moon shone through the sunroof, highlighting the gold streaks in his auburn hair. His wide-set eyes were a stormy grey in the pearly light and a day's growth of stubble shadowed his square jaw.

"And I am careful, that's why you're driving me, I won't know exactly where she is until I get closer." Staring out of the passenger window, his low mutter barely reached her. "And I don't know what I'll find, I may need a healer."

So there it was. She was a means to an end.

The worry for Jess equally matched the hurt of being used. Her stomach dropped as the lump caught in her throat, and she fought the sudden burn of hot tears. It shouldn't hurt.

But it did. He hadn't come to her because he knew she loved Thea and Jess. She just suited his purpose.

Directing her down a side road, he peered into the darkness.

As they'd hit the outskirts of the city, the clear sky turned, filling with voluminous rain clouds that rapidly started to pour, lashing the streets and hampering visibility.

Dread and panic all but consumed him. Something was wrong. Something was very wrong.

The museum was shrouded in shadow.

The palpable hum of Dillon O'Leary's magic hung in the air, but like this whole situation, there was something distinctly *off* about it.

At his grunted, "This'll do." Ellie braked, jerking him against his seatbelt. Yanking the wheel she manoeuvred the little car tight up against a row of trade wheelie bins and turned off the engine, before studying the exterior of the building.

"There's cameras at the second floor level all the way along, can you do something about them?" Her voice whispered, her blue eyes were luminescent, nerves and worry clear on her face as she sat, waiting for him. Gods' she was lovely.

Lowering the window he whispered low, holding his closed hand to his lips. Letting the words thrum in his palm until the magic was too strong to hold, he opened his grasp, and blew the spell towards the building.

The dim security lights blinked out, and the cameras nodded to the floor, as if sleeping.

As he struggled from the ridiculously low car, Ellie came to stand beside him. It was just the same as that first time; she was a lightning rod to his magic, amplifying what he could achieve.

The loud clatter down the alley had him instinctively grabbing for her hand, and gripping it tightly, he focused on the swinging door a good distance away. Drawing up magic it rushed through him, right and true. Her hand in his hummed, power bouncing between them.

The hazing was different with her hand in his, there was no sensation of fracturing, it was warm and fizzy.

And fast.

They regained corporeal form in a millisecond in front of the fire-escape. Her erratic breathing was the first thing to reach him, and he turned, gripping her arms, unconsciously steadying her. "Are you okay?"

Her lips managed a small smile as she tried to nod, and he found himself smiling back. "Okay then."

The swinging doors clattered back against the sandstone as he stepped over the threshold into the dark museum.

The hallway stretched ahead, echoing with sounds of wind and rain, and tension settled over him. Closing his eyes he let his surroundings tip into him, searching for any trace of what had happened.

Malice ripped through him, emotions teeming one on top of the other, too many for him to decipher. Burning heat rose instantly, filling him with rage, the need to fight, to protect. His hands gripped his head as he tried to pull out, tried to throw his barriers back up. He was losing it.

"Adam..." Ellie's whisper was small, and high as she called his name. At the revulsion filling her voice and the burn filling him, he almost couldn't bring himself to turn around.

But she was afraid, her fear like a beacon, and he managed a leaden, faltering step towards her.

As his gaze fastened on her, he knew the image she made would never leave him, it would be forever seared into his mind.

The moon shone down, her hair shining silver in the ghostly light. Her wide blue eyes the only thing visible above her hands as she'd covered her mouth, to muffle her shocked cry.

Blood was all around her, splattered and smeared on the concrete. The loom of the museum protected the grotesque leavings from the rain, and as the wind chased the clouds across the sky, the intermittent moonlight glinted against something beside her.

All at once he was with her, no thought of how, he was just there, in the circle of what appeared to be a violent slaughter. Bending to grab the object from the floor, he rose, clasping her. Pulling her to him, hiding her face from the ugliness.

The silky length of her hair warmed his palm as he cupped her head, and looking into the museum, he hazed them inside.

The darkness was oppressive, their breaths rasping against the weight of it. Whatever he'd picked up from the floor, he shoved in his pocket, unnoticed. His only thought was Ellie.

The length of her was plastered to him, his hand splayed across the flair of her hip. The sweet scent of summer on the ocean was all around her, filling his senses, calming him.

Her hands settled on his chest as she looked up at him, the top of her head barely reaching his jaw.

Her blue eyes were stark and wide, and locked with his.

He was *supposed* to protect her, to cherish her. To know her scent, her taste... The certainty of it, pouring through him, was frightening.

She felt like home, exactly as she had that day in the ocean, the feel of her soft thigh had been lush in his grasp, the water had made her dark lashes spiky.

But then wasn't now, and he'd waited long enough.

"Adam, it wasn't, all that blood... it's not—"

"I know it's not, Jess." And with that surety in his mind, he lowered his lips to hers.

Hers were soft, and he found himself gentling his embrace, smoothing his palms down her arms, drawing her closer, wrapping himself around her, as he finally learnt her.

She was a balmy ocean breeze and a hot summer night all at once. Sending desire racing through him.

Sweeping his tongue softly against her lips, he groaned at the decadent feel of her.

Her hands fisted his shirt, and she must've gone on tiptoe, as she lifted to deepen their kiss.

The slow exploration answered what felt like a lifetime of questions, but the main one lingered in his mind as he slowly lifted his head to look down at her; they'd go off like dynamite together.

Confused arousal clouded her expression as she opened her mouth to speak.

'Adam—"

Shaking his head he cut her off. "This isn't the time." Feeling a twang of guilt at what must have sounded like a brush off, he tightened his arms around her as she tried to pull away. "My fault. Something's wrong, can't you feel it?"

She frowned at his words, stepping from his embrace.

Her teeth pressed into her bottom lip as she looked down the long corridor. Surprising him again when she faced him with a nod. "You're right. We need to figure out what's going on. But I can tell you now, Jess isn't here. She's doesn't seem to be *anywhere*, I can't get any sense of her."

CHAPTER 3

THE CERTAINTY IN HER WORDS, confirmed his own feelings. But still...

"How do you know she's not here?" His head tipped as he questioned her. He'd known Jess wasn't there the minute they'd stepped foot inside. She'd been here alright, and in the last hour or so. But how did Ellie know?

Ellie lifted her chin as she spoke, and he couldn't fathom out what he was missing in her words.

"I *know* when any of the three of you are close by, and when you're not."

Making their way further into the museum, she self-consciously tugged at her sweater, before tucking her hair behind one ear. "And if you know she's not here, then why did we come all this way?" She planted her hands on her hips as spoke, clearly exasperated and a little flustered.

Giving in to the voice that had been nagging at him, he decided she was entitled to know certain things. Who knew, maybe she'd feel inclined to return the gesture.

Coming to a standstill, he stood heavier on his good leg, to ease the ache of the other. Spreading his hands in supplication, he released a sigh. "Okay, so when I did a location spell for her, this was the last place it could find her. I needed someone I trusted to get me up here in a hurry, because I also saw a vampire." He rushed through the last words, hoping she focused more on 'vampire' and less on *trusted*.

Ellie took a stuttering step back at his words. "Be still my heart, 'trust' no less." Her left eyebrow arched as she stopped to stare at him. "I've already brought you up here, you don't need to go throwing around empty words. Can you pick anything else up now?"

He sighed, choosing not to explain that he did trust her. "The last thing she did was throw up protective barriers, cloaking herself from everyone. As long as those barriers remain up, I know she's alright. I just have to find her." He rolled his eyes at that thought, gesturing again down the dark corridor. "And by figuring out what the hell has gone on here, I might work out where she'd go."

Just hearing himself say the words out loud helped. She'd cloaked herself, ergo she was safe. *Good lass.* What had felt like an uncontainable mix of panic and rage that had been pumping through him back in the bay, had eased as soon as they'd got in the car. And it had all but dissipated at the realisation that Jess did indeed have the power, and the knowledge, to protect herself. He'd left easily detectable signs, with metaphysical markers that he was still in the bay. Surely she'd be headed for home, to get help?

There was no light shining at any point ahead of them, no alarms, no security lighting, nothing. Jess must've absolutely fried the circuits in this place.

He casually looked down at Ellie as they kept walking; being ninety-nine percent sure that Jess was safe, and walking through what was clearly a display of some pretty heavy-duty Lavelle magic left him almost happy. It certainly left him calm enough to focus on the matter at hand.

"And don't think for a minute that I'm letting go the fact that you *know* when we're close, and you *know* she's off grid. We're circling back around to that, for sure. Just, after this, okay?"

Slowly considering his words, Ellie decided it was time to even the playing field. "Fine. But you want me to explain and answer your questions? Then you'll have to answer mine. And I have *lots.*" Any moonlight that had been shining through the busted fire escape door ended abruptly as the door slammed shut. His warm hand grabbed hers as the gasp left her lips, and her heart just about beat out of her chest as they were plunged into all-consuming darkness.

It was hollow and cold, like being lost in a void. The only certainty was her hand in his.

Sliding her phone from the back pocket of her jeans, she hit the home button, siding up for her torch, groaning at the low battery sign. "It'll give us light for a bit at any rate..."

Her voice faded away as a warm glow emanated from beside her. He'd lifted his other hand before him, and was whispering a soft chant. The words were deep and quiet; a hush warming the blackness. It was as if dust motes had come to life, little embers that glowed and fizzed. Spinning his finger, they circled, growing in numbers, and with a flick of his wrist he sent them into the air above them. They lit the corridor, keeping pace as they walked.

She could feel his magic on her skin, his low voice easing through her, and her heart-rate took on a deep, heavy, cadence, heating her blood.

Why was it only him that made her feel this way?

Her hand was still held firmly by his, and the flickering light cast shapes on the sandstone walls, like the shadows of crows wings. The smell of the rain-filled night swept along the corridor, and the secrets of the one hundred and sixty year old museum whispered within the walls.

The sound of the wind came from all angles, covering their footsteps, as they approached what seemed to be a central point. Marble steps led down, and moonlight became visible again as it peered through skylights and windows.

Fresh night air just teased her senses, and Ellie couldn't decipher where it was coming from as they walked further into the maze of the museum.

Staring into each doorway and along each corridor, she couldn't see anything out of place. She frowned in confusion.

"Do you have any idea what we're looking for? I mean, Jess isn't here. Apart from the gruesome goings-on in the alleyway there's nothing to see." She mulled her words over, and turned to look at Adam. "Do you think that's why you saw a vampire in your vision? To symbolise all the blood?"

Adam stopped, pulling her up short. His upper body was leant forward, as if intently listening for something, but he turned to her, a questioning look on his face. "What do you mean a symbol?" Gold still flecked his eyes, and they didn't have that frost in them, like they normally did when he looked at her. *His eyes weren't cold when he kissed you, either.*

Shaking off that thought, she firmly pushed it to the back of her mind. That was going in the 'to-be-dealt-with-later' box. That would need her full attention—after they knew where Jess was.

"I mean, you saw Jess. And there's all that blood." Ellie shuddered at the memory of how the tinny smell had assaulted her senses, and looking down to find herself stood almost in the pool of it. "Maybe Jess witnessed a mugging gone wrong?

Vampires represent blood, maybe that's what it was trying to tell you. And maybe we should be trying to phone her again, or checking police stations, and not breaking into museums that could end up with us getting arrested?!" Exasperation filled her voice as she spoke. With each word logic and common sense poured through her. This was madness, she was still shocked, and overemotional and angry about what had happened earlier on the beach. She must've taken leave of her bloody senses! They'd broken into a museum for goodness sakes.

Pulling her hand from his, she stood in front of him, planting it on her hip, wrenching her hair out of her face with the other. "I must be nuts. This is London, it's a lot more likely that Jess is caught up in regular crime, and nothing magical at all." She gestured around them, "Adam, you realise we're *trespassing* in the bloody Victoria and Albert Museum!"

The rhythmic clicking that tapped at her subconscious grew louder as she stared at him. Adrenaline was making itself known, pumping through her as she turned towards the noise, elevating the sound of her heart, pounding in her ears.

Time seemed to slow as she moved, but she was aware that her hair had whipped around her face to settle across her shoulders, as Adam's barely audible whisper of her name reached her.

Staring at the cold marble floor, she waited for the cause of the noise to appear, unable to stop the shaking of her hands as unexplainable fear battered her.

Even the light seemed to retreat, the clouds covered the moon, and the golden glow that had been accompanying them stayed behind, lending only the smallest glimmer.

Sounds began to match the rhythm of what her mind was trying to tell her was footsteps. Breathing... panting.

She must have taken a faltering step back, as Adam's hands gripped her upper arms, hard enough to leave bruises, as he tried to push her behind him.

But not before her gaze clashed with unholy blue eyes, they glowed from within the black face.

Fur and fangs, so much, so big...

Ellie struggled to process what she was seeing, as the

enormous black wolf rounded the corner. The muzzle pulled back to reveal long white canines, while a deep rumble lifted from its chest.

The ears were back, and its hackles were raised. As if the creature needed to appear bigger. It was huge, and Ellie felt her breath fade away as her head spun.

Barely keeping her footing, Adam swept her behind him, and she stepped back as he flicked his hands out at his sides.

Amber glowed down the vein tracery of his forearms, pooling into his palms, as it sparked and caught, engulfing his hands in burning balls of flames. He moved forward, slowly lifting his hands higher, bringing them before him, warning the wolf.

Fire reflected in the preternatural gaze, and the wolf almost seemed to grin, his ears lifting from their flattened position. The beast took a step back, sitting on his hunches, looking for all the world like it was pleased to see them.

Adam's hands faltered, lowering slightly, his head tilting as he stared at the enormous animal.

Easing around Adam, she looked in wonder, her hectic breathing and pounding heart still the only thing she could hear. He seemed *familiar* somehow and, unsure of what she was doing, she took a small step closer, while the wolf tilted his head, watching her.

The ripple across his back stopped her in her tracks, as he slowly lay down, the fur receding before her eyes, leaving a smooth expanse of tanned, muscled *man.*

He shook his head, shaking back the silky fall of black hair as he came to his feet, naked as the day he was born.

"Jason!" Adam's shocked voice had her rapidly raising her eyes back to his face, as opposed to everything else that was visible, where she met his grinningly flirtatious gaze.

She opened and closed her mouth, finally closing it again, swallowing against the dryness. Holding her hands wide, she raised her brows, looking back to Adam and then forward at Jess's very naked best friend.

"I...?" She'd have liked to have formed words at this point, but simply couldn't get her brain to respond.

"And hello to you, Ellie. Adam." Jason pointed at his hands. "Are you gonna put those things out, man? You're heating the place up."

The slight chuckle that accompanied his words made Ellie catch her breath, hysterical laughter bubbled up within her, as she shook her head. Bending at the waist, she put her hands on her knees, sucking in deep breaths as relief swept through her. Her hair hung around her, almost touching the marble as she braced herself, while she tried to evaluate if she'd be better to just sit on the floor before she keeled over.

A noise behind her was accompanied by warm hands on her shoulders, and she found herself being eased back into a softly upholstered carver chair. Pushing the hair back from her face she opened her eyes to meet Jason's still glowing blue gaze at point blank range.

He was rubbing her chilled upper arms, encouraging warmth back into her.

"You okay?" His voice was gruff, still cracking and returning to normal. Heat emanated from his hands—from all of him, as he kept watching her, until she rapidly nodded.

"I'm good... I'm, phew. Gimme a minute."

Giving her a smile, he touched her cheek. "Gotcha, been quite a day for you." Lifting his gaze to Adam's, Ellie watched it ice over. "It's almost like Adam shouldn't be dragging you into this." As he stood fully, she found herself faced with a very personal view of his nakedness, and the choked sound she must've made had him stepping back, firing a quick look of apology her way. "Sorry, babe."

Pulling another chair out from under a nearby desk, he stood behind it. From what Ellie could tell, it was entirely for her benefit, as being naked clearly didn't bother him at all. *And nor should it, no siree.* Inwardly rolling her eyes at her libido, she sat up straighter in her chair, waiting as Adam came forward.

"Jason?" As he walked passed Ellie, he shook the flames from his hands, banking the fire. Streaks of soot raced up his arms, before sinking into his skin, fading away to nothing, as did his quietly spoken words. "You're a wolf."

Ellie watched the two of them; it was surreal as they faced each other, an ornate chair between them. Adam with his leg encased in a boot and a charred t-shirt, and Jason, leaning on the back of the chair, naked.

The look he levelled at Adam wasn't exactly friendly, and she found herself holding her breath.

"Guilty."

Adam continued to stare, before finally shaking his head, hard. "I had no idea. Does Jess know?"

Jason merely raised his brows at Adam before nodding towards Ellie. "What do you think? Jess will bust you up for dragging Ellie into this, what the bloody-hell were you thinking? You've managed to keep Thea, and so you thought, Jess, out of this life for all these years, and tonight you do this." Throwing his hands in the air in frustration he walked away, before turning back, his eyes iridescent in their anger. "How do you think you're going to keep Thea out of it now?!"

Ellie frowned, desperately trying to process what she was hearing, but nothing made any sense. "Keep Thea out of what?" As they both turned to look at her, she raised her hands. "And you don't have to worry, I'd never involve her in anything that could hurt her, or Jess for that matter."

Jason's expression infinitely softened as he looked at her. Lifting a marble bust from the table, he carefully placed it on the floor, before snapping off the white linen table cloth and wrapping it around his hips as he came towards her.

Crouching down, he clasped her hands, offering her a sad smile. "I know you wouldn't, Sweetheart, but it's all too late for that now. Jess is clearly in this—whatever the hell *it* is that's happening, because I'm damned if I know—up to her neck. And after Adam has pulled you in, we have no choices left now. I have to find Jess, and the best thing you can do is go home, and have Adam put some protection on your place. Better yet have Thea do it, Jess tells me her spell casting is infinitely stronger."

Coming to his feet he turned to Adam, holding out his hand. "And, witch, whatever that is in your pocket that reeks of vampire, I suggest you give it to me. It'll act like a bloody homing signal."

Ellie watched cold detachment settle over Adam's features, something she was only used to seeing aimed at herself.

He lifted a brow, as he reached in his pocket, producing a gold cuff. The moonlight caught the dried blood smeared across it as he held it out to Jason.

The wolf's eyes eclipsed Jason's as his nostril flared, and Ellie watched a muscle in his clenched jaw twitch as he stepped closer.

Taking the bangle carefully between his thumb and fore-finger he held it away from himself as he turned. "Come on, I've got to bag this... And get some clothes on."

It was clearly an office that Jess and Jason shared, and looking around Adam couldn't believe his sister had managed to keep this side of her life secret for all these years.

Two roll top desks faced each other, the rain spattered night tapping the wide Victorian sash window on one side, while a low fire crackled in the ceramic and iron fireplace on the other. A notice board virtually covered one wall, with photos and paper clippings of artefacts and relics pinned everywhere.

Staring at it, it took Adam a couple of minutes to decipher what it was; any image with a post-it stuck next it, gave the original location and current location... Jess and Jason were recovering relics with magical properties and returning them to covens and clans for safe keeping.

Some of the images just had post-its with a question mark.

How the hell hadn't he realised?

Ellie was sat calmly in the fireside chair, the warm light from the flames catching the autumn colours of her hair. And he felt confusion wash over him. The life he'd convinced himself his family had was just an illusion.

Keeping them safe had been why he'd left — and it hadn't worked. They'd found trouble anyway.

Fingers of fear and panic brushed his skin, and his anger found focus as Jason came back from getting dressed.

"So this is your setup is it? Sending Jess into the lairs of gods-know what, so you can—what?—put a tick in the box. Or does this pay well?"

Jason's expression was frustratingly calm as he gave Adam a passing glance before walking to Ellie.

He held a large, clear, ziplock bag open as he stopped in front of her. Giving her a small grin and wink, he nodded down at her shoes. "I'm pretty confident that you don't want to wear those home."

Staring down at Ellie's trainers, Adam could make out the fine stain of blood that had soaked into the white soles and probably splashed onto the red leather.

"Toe them off carefully, and I'll pick them up, I don't mind if she comes to find me."

Even Adam couldn't ignore the menace that tinged his words, and despite how angry he was at Jason for dragging Jess into this, it was more important that they nullified the threat. As quickly as possible.

Rubbing the back of his neck, he turned to stare out the window as he spoke. "The vampire you're looking for is blonde, her hair is long and she travels with an accomplice. But I don't think she's as powerful—or maybe as important as the blonde."

Zipping the bag closed, Jason dropped it on his desk. Before taking the other chair opposite Ellie. "Now you've stopped being a wanker, you have my attention. When did you have a run in with her?"

Spinning back around at the insult, Adam stared him down. "Watch your fucking tone. You dragged my sister into all this. The only reason I'm helping is to try and get this mess sorted out. And when it is—"

Ellie quietly said his name, her blue eyes were sad under her raised brows as she looked at him. "Do you think, you could just not do *this* right now. The two of you can shout and bloody scream later, from what I can gather we're all on the same side. So could you act like it—just this once?"

Opening his mouth to retaliate, he found his breath catch in his throat. What was he supposed to say to that?

He closed it with a snap, and leant back against the edge of Jess's desk.

Closing his eyes and releasing a breath, he nodded, lifting his head to look back up at her. "Of course. Shout later—you're right."

The look of surprise that flashed across her face at his agreement, left him wondering how big a dick he'd been to her all these years, if decent logical behaviour from him was enough to shock her.

His most recent dream had told him, very clearly, he would be facing old transgressions. He hadn't figured Ellie would be at the top of that list; after all, he'd done so many stupid things, the list had grown considerably in the last year alone...

Clasping his hands, he looked at them both. One thing at a time, that was all he could do now. "I've never met her—the vampire, but sometimes I dream. I don't always know why initially, but then it sort-of works out, to a message or a warning."

Pushing his hair back with a sweep of his hand, he tried to order his thoughts, to make sure he was as accurate as possible. "It would've been August when I had the first one, before this." He gestured disgustedly down at the boot encasing his leg. "Then Friday last week, then last night. The first dream was in a park, there was a big fountain... swans, like a fairytale."

"Was it day or night?" Jason spoke slowly, and Adam refocused his gaze, looking at Jess's best friend. They'd been friends since school, over ten

years. How long had she known about the wolf?

"Er, night. Why?"

"Anything else stand out?" Jason's tone was more curious than anything else, and left Adam with the distinct impression that he was holding back.

"The smell of lavender, I've never been so struck by scent in a dream, but it was overpowering. What aren't you telling me?"

Giving a regal wave, Jason urged him on. "Keep going, it's all starting to make sense."

"The creature was in the undergrowth, waiting. I couldn't be sure what it was at first. But she's slim, blonde, lots of skin on display. Her eyes were red, deep red."

Looking sightlessly up at the ceiling, with its rose light mouldings and fine filigree works, he let his mind drift. "The other two dreams were the same. Two vampires, one blonde, one dark. The dark one is weaker somehow, subservient maybe, I couldn't figure it out. But there was blood, and a lot of it. And a wolf,"—looking back to Jason, he tilted his head —"which I now know is you."

"Okay, so not dreams then: visions." Jason rose, pacing to the fire, frowning as he seemed to mull over his thoughts.

"If you want to call them visions, fine. But they're not reliable enough for me to act before hand, some of them come to nothing."

"Hmm, I wonder about that." Absently stoking the fire, Jason lifted his gaze to Adam. "Jess was in St. James's Park in August. It was the first time it attacked her. St. James's is home to the Tiffany Fountain."

Pushing from the desk, Adam hobbled to the window, shaking his head. "Bloody portent, what good is it if I'm not shown the most important part?"

Pressing his forehead to the cold glass, he closed his eyes. Tired of magic, tired of the struggle. "Jess will most likely be on her way home to the bay, once this is sorted I want her out of this Jason. Out of this life. I want them safe."

Jason's derisive laugh grated against his nerves, sending sparks firing beneath his skin.

"Why would she go back to the bay? Thea isn't there."

Clenching his fists he turned, "Thea has nothing to do with this!" His voice rose, filling the room. "And where else would she go?"

Jason shook his head, his brows lifting sarcastically. "You're such an idiot, I almost can't believe it. But then, this is you, Adam, so I shouldn't be surprised. You really don't get it, do you?"

Jason's eyes had started to churn the bright blue of his wolf.

As his own blood heated beneath his skin, Adam was sure his own eyes answered in turn. "I clearly don't seem to be *getting* a lot tonight—so why don't you spell it out for me."

Jason's tone was icy cold and soft when he spoke. "She

wouldn't go back to the bay because there's no-one there who can help her."

"I'm there!" His voice all but roared as he shouted back, taking a step towards Jason.

"How? You've told her you don't *use* your magic. She wouldn't go home purposely. To protect *you!*" Jason yelled back at him, the sharp points of his canines visible now, as his lips curled in rage.

The words hit him like a freight train, but Jason was still yelling.

"You're so bloody busy being the mighty Adam Lavelle, so sure that you can *fix* everything. Patting Jess and Thea on the head like 'good girls'—well here's a news flash for you, buddy, you telling them you don't use *your* magic, doesn't mean that they don't use THEIRS!"

Truly angry now, Jason closed in on him, grabbing Adam by a handful of his t-shirt. "And as for me dragging Jess into this, you couldn't have it more wrong."

Adam grabbed Jason in return, the scorching burn flooding his palms, and the acrid smell of scorching fabric lifted between them as Jason's shirt singed and smoked.

"And if you want to know more than that, you can ask her your bloody self. But be sure that she'll have questions for you too. Are you prepared to answer those? Are you prepared to tell them the truth?"

Locked in each other's grip, they stared at each other, breathing hard. The eyes of the wolf darted warily at the fire that lived in Adam's gaze.

Adam didn't know how long they stood there, rage coursing through him. It was only as he became aware of Ellie stepping cautiously towards them.

Placing a hand on each of them, she waited.

The cool, almost rhythmic feel of her touch was mesmerically calming as her voice reached him.

64

"That's enough, both of you."

The breath he felt her take was as placid as the morning tide, rolling slowly through him, and he felt his grip on Jason lessen.

Her touch more than placated the wolf; Adam watched Jason's blue gaze deepen, become languid. It reminded him of Murphy...

Breaking away, he fully let Jason go, shrugging off her touch.

He kept his mouth firmly closed, unsure if he'd yell at her for touching him, or beg her never to stop.

In the last few hours everything he was sure of was being swept away. What else didn't he understand?

Taking a few more steps back for good measure, Adam turned to Ellie. Guilt and shame bled through him, Jason was right... "I shouldn't have asked you to bring me here, I shouldn't have dragged you into this."

Stunned, Ellie stood stock-still. It wasn't an outright apology, but holy-hell it was probably the closest thing she was ever going to get from Adam.

The flames that had sparked so suddenly to life in his gaze when Jason had grabbed him, were banked now. Leaving his summer-sky blue irises behind. Long gone was the flirtatious light from years ago. Now he stood before her, his face drawn, his gaze holding a bomb-blast expression of a man that couldn't take much more.

But there was more, so much more. And they were all going to have to deal with it. And they could start with something she was becoming more sure of with each thing he said.

"Adam, when you have these dreams, are Thea and Jess *ever* in them?"

He seemed to brace himself as he digested her words, slowly shaking his head. "No. Why?" They had been, but only once, and he wasn't prepared to share it.

On a sigh, Ellie looked from Adam to Jason. "I think the dreams *want* to alert you when your sisters need help. But they can't."

"Alert me how?" His voice was sad, defeated. And she hated dealing him another blow. But it was time he came to fully realise how his actions had left his sisters no choice but to isolate him.

"You convinced them Adam; that you didn't use your magic. I think they suspected, but certainly not to the level I've seen you use it in the last day. It was years ago now, just after you left the bay. Jess and Thea created a blocking spell, so anything they did or any being that was drawn to them or their magic was hidden from you, to keep you safe."

"How do you know? How do you know this?" He was shaking his head, his brow furrowed, pain etched his features, and Ellie hurt for him.

"Because they needed someone they trusted to act as an anchor on this plain for the spell to work. Thea asked for my help."

Jason's voice carried quietly across the room. "And Jess asked for mine."

CHAPTER 4

"NOT THAT I think you deserve it, but why haven't you asked her to heal you?" Jason nodded down at his leg, keeping his voice soft.

Ellie had gone to scrub any trace of blood from her hands, and to check nothing had soaked into her socks or jeans. Adam kept his eyes on the door to the washroom, unsure if he should tell Jason the truth.

"It's not a mortal break." Mentally shrugging to himself at the cryptic response, he sighed and leant back in the fireside chair. It was all he was prepared to share. No point dressing it up.

"Going to expand on that?" Jason dropped into the chair facing him.

"Nope."

Watching the fire, Jason stretched out his legs. "What are you going to do now?"

"I have no idea." *Ain't that the truth?* "As you've proved tonight, I know nothing about either of my sister's lives. I have no idea who she'd go to for help. The only thing I'm sure of, is that she wouldn't go to Yorkshire."

With a shake of his head, Jason spread his hands wide. "And what has Jess got against the rolling dales?"

"Thea is there. With Marc and his family. The only thing I know for sure is that she won't risk Ellie's family."

The door made a hushing noise as it closed behind Ellie. "I agree. I think that bears repeating." She gave him the smallest smile as she came towards them. "I agree with you Adam, Jess won't go there."

Sliding her hands in the pockets of her dark jeans, she rocked back on her socked feet. "But Thea might know where she would go. And asking her all depends on whether you're still running around with this daft notion that you're strong enough to deal with everything, and they can't handle anything."

There was no edge to her voice as she spoke. She merely said what she had to say and waited him out.

Feeling edgy and confined, but too tired to drag himself back to his feet and stand on his aching leg, he rubbed his fingers hard into his brow. As if he could push out the throbbing headache that resided there.

"I can't just drop this on her, Ellie." He held his hands up, to the room in general as both Jason and Ellie opened their mouths to shout him down. "I have to talk with them, to tell them *all of it*, I know that. But the chances are Jess would deliberately go somewhere none of us would think of until she'd made up her mind."

"You gotta point there." Jason looked speculative as he rubbed his palms up and down the arms of the leather chair. "She's ornery enough, and bloody minded enough to do just that—no idea where she gets that from, by the way."

The glint of humour in his eye was the first crack Adam had seen in him tonight. And he found himself grateful that he still had a chance at friendship with the big bastard. "Thanks."

Leaning forward, he braced his forearms on his knees, loosely clasping his hands, and stared into the fire. He let the flames dance before him as he threw out the gossamer strands of his magic. Breathing fluidly, focusing on keeping firm yet gentle control.

He picked up Thea's essence, the moist air and the ancient energy of the old city of York filled him.

"Thea and Marc are safe. In York, just where they're supposed to be." He murmured the words slowly, careful not to break his concentration. Before trying again, this time to find Jess.

She was there, her energy, her life-force, but just beyond his reach. It was like he was looking into a fog. Her magic was so strong that he couldn't even tap at the edges of the casting. Couldn't even request that she let him in.

How hadn't he realised she'd become so powerful. There was only one other witch he could think of with that kind of juice, and he'd be contacting her as soon as he got back to the bay.

Leaning back, he turned his palms to the ceiling, letting any remnant of magic fizz in his hands and lift into the ether.

"She's safe, that's all I can get. Her barriers are up. Hard. If she was in danger or distressed I'd feel the tremor, I'd be able to work my way in somehow."

Ellie released a breath as he spoke, he felt her ever-so-soft exhale from the left of him.

"So what do we do now?"

"You both go back to the bay." Jason's answer was firm, as if he was ready to argue his point.

"Agreed."

"I mean it, Adam, you're a bloody liability with that leg, and I won't have you drag Ellie across London, into gods know what."

"You're right."

"If you'd—" Jason stopped mid-sentence to stare at him. "What?"

"I said I agree, you're right. Does that bear repeating too?" Stretching anyway he could, to try and lessen the throbbing of his head, shoulders, leg... Well, you name it, everything bloody well hurt. "You can cover more on foot than I can, for one. And two, truthfully; I'm not convinced she's even in London anymore, and I can do far better tracking her back in the bay, from my one home. And three, I want to get Ellie back there. I can cloak the bay, it's smaller, and I'll be able to energetically detect any changes or unwelcome visitors a hell of a lot sooner than here."

Jason shook his head, and looked up at Ellie. "Has he had a blow to the head? He's being reasonable... Did you hear that?"

Ellie managed a laugh, exhaustion shadowed her eyes, and he detected the slightest tremor in her lips as they curved. Somewhere in amongst all this, he'd finally begun to accept that he couldn't keep behaving like a bastard to keep her out of his way. He was going to have to face the pull between them.

"Ellie, will you take us home?"

Her answer was instant. "Of course. Now?"

He tried to make sure his gratitude showed on his face. "Yes, please." Her eyes were wide and unsure as their gaze held, and he found he had no words to ease her uncertainty.

"Well then, that's that sorted. Let's get you two kids on the road." Jason's cheery tone had them both turning startled eyes to his. And his mumbled, "All I do is play Cupid," was lost on them, as Adam pushed to his feet.

"What about you? What are you doing next?" Adam leant heavily on the back of the chair, as he spoke.

Jason shrugged, pushing his hands into his pockets. "The bangle reeks of vampire, so now I have a scent to track. But I figure wherever the scourge is, Jess won't be. So I'll head for her, and wait for you to find Jess, if anything changes, I'll let you know."

Jason shut the door on the little Mini and waited, watching them drive down the alley and out onto the street, before looking up at the nearly full hunter moon, it was just about visible in the early morning sky.

He needed answers from Jess before tracking the vampire-scourge. And thanks to the mix of blood on the bangle, he was starting to get a better idea of what was going on.

He hadn't been back to the bay in months, it was long beyond time.

~

ELLIE TIREDLY WATCHED the traffic edge forward as they sat in a queue of crawling cars, waiting to get on the M25.

Trying to get out of London, at the start of the morning rush hour, as everyone else was trying to get in had proved time consuming. The whole journey was usually only an hour and a half, give or take, but it had taken that long just to get to the outskirts of the city today.

She breathed a sigh of relief at the first sign for Guildford, switching lanes and following the southbound junction, relieved when the traffic eased out. She put the little Mini through its paces, so great was her need to get home to the mid-morning tide, and hear the rattle of sails hanging on the air.

Adam's eyes were closed, and he breathed evenly. The night had been a wave of revelations for him, she supposed. For her too. Jason in his wolf form flashed in her mind, and she found herself softly chuckling. She'd known there were *other* things out there, but she'd kind-of assumed they came in

71

human form. She knew there were other covens of witches, and solitary practitioners, healers and seers. She'd heard of a demon family living in the Lake District. From what she understood, other than a pretty substantial appetite, and being preternaturally strong, they were just like everyone else.

But wolves and vampires... She'd known they existed, once. As in 'once upon a time,' but had assumed that centuries of war and the shift into *modern times* had largely wiped them out.

Silly now, she knew. Magic existed, energy could be moulded, and thoughts did move mountains. So there was room for anything to survive. She'd always wondered about Jason, known there was something *extra* about him. She just hadn't figured he was a lycanthrope.

"You're thinking is loud. I'd've thought your mind was a quiet, peaceful place."

Adam's gruff words made her jerk in her seat, as she whipped a quick look at him. His eyes were still closed, he features calm and relaxed.

"I thought you were asleep."

Grey October daylight had fought back the night. Its weak light left the feeling of being stuck in a half-world. The quiet inside the car, and the constant thrum of the engine had lulled her into a contemplative state.

"Nah, not with your mind churning the way it is. The energy's too busy in here. What'cha worrying over?"

He'd slowly opened his eyes as he spoke, turning to face her, still resting against the headrest. His voice was croaky from the silence and lack of sleep, it was also friendly.

She had no idea what to do with a *friendly* Adam. The lack of animosity was odd and unsettling. "Why are you being nice?"

Slightly shocked by her own words, she felt the burn of discomfort at his laugh. *Here we go, back to normal...*

"I've been that much of a bastard, huh?"

No 'here we go'? Ellie kept both hands on the steering wheel, and concentrated on the road ahead. Firmly setting her lips, she frowned at his response. He was like Jekyll and Hyde, and not knowing what to expect was exhausting.

"Adam, yesterday evening I was stood waist deep in the freezing ocean while we yelled at each other. Since then you've yelled at me some more, blamed me for your magic, and all your family's magical problems, decided you needed a healer and *'I'd do,'* and now you want me to share my worries. And you wonder why I'm leery."

"I've also kissed you."

The words dropped between them, and Ellie found herself clenching the wheel tighter still. What the hell was she supposed to say to that?

Making a small sound of frustration in the back of throat, she tutted at him, shaking her head. "I'm not even going near that. I'm tired of *this* Adam; you blaming me, for years. Your icy disdain, *for years!* And now being... I don't know... almost *friendly?* And asking me nicely to bring you home. I. Don't. Even. Know. You're like an emotional barometer when a storm's rolling in. I just—"

"You're right."

"What?" Temper and frustration littered her voice. The signs for Petersfield came into view, and she lifted a sigh of thanks to the Gods. *Nearly home.* She'd drop him to his house, then she'd take five bloody minutes to sift all this through her mind before getting some sleep. A good twelve, or even fifteen, lazy hours. While her body and her emotions recouped.

"I said you're right. I am—was—angry at you for what you did; for what happened. But I do know it wasn't deliberate." His brow furrowed as he said quietly, "And it isn't lost on me that Jason and Jess were friends before the magic. And I'm also not that big-of-a schmuck to ignore the fact that with no magic, she could've been caught up in all this anyway, without a way to protect herself." He seemed to struggle to find the words.

He twisted in his seat, before finally throwing up his hands. "My own sisters magically blocked me out Ellie. I-I'm trying to process that. And being a wanker to you isn't... it just doesn't... I'm done with it. Does that make any sense at all?"

She felt the confused honesty in his words. And had no idea what to do with them. "Not really no. And having seen your *magic* at work, I know you're most definitely blocking them; what's good for one, and all that." Releasing a long sigh, she stifled a yawn, keeping the little Mini racing down the A3 towards home. "We have to talk about this." The sense of change had been hanging in the air since the Thunder Moon, but its energy had ramped up since Adam had been back in the bay. It was time to deal with the past, not only for her and Adam, but Thea and Jess too. Ellie just wanted a little alone time to gather her thoughts first. "But now isn't the time, we need to wait for Jess to surface. Which means we can both get some rest, because once Thea and Jess are home, I have a feeling this isn't going to be quick or easy."

"Fine. But I'm not going home. Take me back to yours."

As they'd hit the traffic coming out of London, he had fallen asleep, the traffic was gridlocked across the M25, and he just couldn't keep his eyes open. The dream had started again. Every time he drifted off it was there, waiting for him.

Both his sisters, and Jason, Marc, Ellie and Lucy all stood together, asking where he was. They were on the deck of his boat, and he was just a few metres away in the ocean.

He was shouting for them to help him.

But they couldn't hear him. The water was cold and dark,

and something brushed by him, but he couldn't swim away, couldn't move.

He could hear them, asking what he'd been doing. Or where he'd been going. Like they never knew where he'd be, like they couldn't rely on him.

Eventually they hauled anchor and sailed away. Leaving him in the echoing dark.

The wind whipped around him, and the sea became more and more vast.

If you remain hidden, you can't be seen. Truth is the light in the dark.

Own your past.

Or it will own you.

Fear clamped a hand round his heart. Squeezing. As the same words carried through him on a cold wind, making his breath catch, as he slowly drifted back to consciousness. He let his thoughts play behind his closed eyes as she continued driving south.

He was trying, desperately trying, to own the decisions he'd made. Even without the dream wearing him down, making him face himself, just getting through each day right now was a kick in the guts. Did Thea and Jess think he'd abandoned them?

He'd blamed Ellie for waking his magic. But that magic had been *his* all along, and he hadn't done much to help himself over the years...

He kept his eyes closed as he took easy breaths, trying to sort his thoughts, as waves of exhaustion reached him. But not his own, Ellie's. A waterfall of emotion bounced from her; her thoughts must be in disarray. She'd come face to face with a werewolf.

It was time for him to try harder to right his mistakes.

"You're thinking is loud. I'd've thought your mind was a quiet, peaceful place."

CHAPTER 5

THE TURNING for her house came into view, and she continued past it, driving across the old bridge and onto the island. Ellie was glad of her car's tinted windows, as Adam pooled power into his palms. The gold flecks of his magic created a sphere of energy, with purple lavender flecks dancing about inside.

His hushed murmur breathed across her skin as he chanted the spell.

Desire shimmered through her as she drove down the quiet roads. Raw energy filled the confines of the car. Her blood heated, pounding, and her palms became clammy as they held the wheel, so great was his effect on her.

Jess's house was right at the bottom of a quaint, and thankfully sleepy, road. Her car was on the drive; where it normally was when she worked in the city.

Blocking Jess's drive, Ellie hopped out, hurrying to her front door and ringing the bell. The late October sun had beaten back the grey, with a helping hand of brisk winds from the English Channel. Leaving the afternoon fresh, with a high, bright sky.

Cupping her hands she peered through the glazed porch window. The place looked deserted.

Heading back to the car, Adam had opened his window. Lifting his hand he let the sparkling orb go.

"As she returns,
Reveal it to me,
As I will it,
So mote it be."

A metaphysical push sent the spell it on its way.

As the orb hit the centre of the front door, it disintegrated into a gentle shimmer, sparks settling on the doorstep.

"She's not here, the place is locked up tight, and she's put up strong protection barriers; smart girl."

"You ever think you haven't given Jess or Thea enough credit?"

Turning solemn eyes to her, Ellie had expected a cutting reply. But his quietly spoken, "It would seem so" left her heart hurting for him.

She really wanted to be able to hate him... On a sigh, she turned the ignition.

No she didn't, she just wanted him not to matter.

But he did. She knew how much he loved his sisters, knew how much this was hurting him.

And whatever had sparked to life between, as they'd swayed off the back of his boat all those years ago, was still there. Waiting.

Holding the car door open wide, she still couldn't believe they were parked outside of her house. She just wanted to be alone, dammit!

Pain caused his brow to furrow as he came to his feet, and the nagging need to help him churned in her gut. Banking it down, she took out her keys and waited for him to slowly make his way to the front door.

Unlike Jess and Adam's houses, the little bay didn't have the benefit of wide open ocean to blow the cobwebs away. The sea had crept in, but was hidden. Only the hollow sound of the slow waves echoing in the fog hinted at its presence.

She took one last longing look down the road towards the shore, as he eased passed her and went into the living room, before closing and bolting the front door.

The chill air encouraged a fine shiver to run through her, and she rubbed her scratchy eyes, pushing her hair back from her face as she went to find him.

He was sat in her comfy grey armchair in the corner, taking in the room. White built-in dressers sat in the alcoves, either side of the fireplace. They were littered with photos, and knickknacks, crystals and mementos. There was a little light, shaped in the word 'Friends' that Thea had charmed to stay permanently lit. The black and white image of them both in their graduation gowns had caught his eye, leaving Thea wondering if he realised how much of his sisters adult lives he'd missed, with all his travels and gallivanting.

Grabbing a soft cream cushion, she sank onto the sofa, starring down at her socked feet. She'd bloody loved her red trainers, and now they were in evidence with a werewolf. The daft thought brought a small smile to her lips, and as she breathed in her own surroundings, she felt a little bit more normal. A little bit more like the rug hadn't been so firmly pulled out from under her.

"Okay then, let's get my house all squared away, magically speaking. Then I'll take you home, and we can both get some rest."

"I'm not going home— not until I'm happy your house is protected."

She raised her brows at the finality in his voice. Like hell he wasn't going home. "Exactly, so let's get on with it." Waving her arm, taking in the room, she looked at him. "I may not be a witch, but I still keep my home energetically clean, and Thea regularly tops up the charms here. Surely you can just top that up?"

Tiredness had long given way to exhaustion. Half-formed thoughts bounced confusedly in his head, his leg throbbed, and Jess's best friend was a werewolf.

A werewolf who's pissed at you for dragging Ellie into this.

He was right too.

Ellie had wrapped her arms around the cushion she held to her body. She'd tucked dainty feet, in black socks underneath her, as she waited for him to answer.

She wasn't going to like it.

A week ago—hell, even yesterday—he wouldn't have considered spending ten minutes with her, let alone ask to sleep in her home. But things were different. Everything had turned on its bloody head, and she'd become an anchor in this storm.

Dark shadows were smudged beneath her eyes.

She was such a pretty little thing. The coppery flecks in her hair brought out her eyes, and years of sailing had left her skin with a fresh honeyed glow. She embodied a sense of peace he only ever found when out on the water.

He felt like a moth, darting closer to her flame. He'd already been singed once. And look at the mess he was in: the rages were getting worse, and harder to control with each bout. He had to dig deeper each time he cast or worked any kind of magic, and his magic was becoming volatile, draining him.

He'd spent years assuming this was how Thea and Jess felt, but after being home since mid-summer he knew better. The problem was with him.

He should've listened when Thea had tried to tell him about the visit from their ancestor, Sarah.

He would listen, when Thea got back, and Jess surfaced, he'd listen. Maybe even explain a few things himself—after he tore a strip off Jess for not mentioning that her best friend was a sodding lykae.

"Adam?" Ellie snapped her fingers, "are you even listening to me?"

Saving those thoughts for later, he looked at her. "Sorry, trying to process it all." Easing forward in the chair, he stretched out his leg. Loosening off the top straps of the boot, he cast his eyes round the room. "Have you got a chair or something, just so I can elevate it for a bit?"

Worry flashed across her face as she came quickly to her feet. The matching footstool was tucked almost out of sight, next to the arm of her chair. The wheels made tracks in the lush carpet, as she pushed it over.

She slid her palm gently under his ankle, slowly taking the weight. Linking her fingers together she made a sling with her hands, carefully settling his leg down.

His breath caught and lodged in his throat, as he watched her. The concentration on her face totally centred on his comfort. Making sure he wasn't in any pain.

The part of his brain that brokered in fear wanted to jerk away from her touch. In case her healing abilities woke anything else up; it wasn't like he didn't have enough to contend with for the minute.

But her power was quiet. Even when she unlinked her fingers, gently touching his lower leg before stepping back.

"Do you want some pain relief?"

She stood in front of him, her hands loosely clasped, hair spilling forward as she worried her full lower lip, while looking at his leg.

"I don't think you trying to help would be a good idea. I

mean, we're only just being civil, and if you tried to heal me who knows what might happen..."

Her brow raised a little higher with each word he spoke. Clearly he was annoying her, but he just couldn't work out the right thing to say to stop digging himself in deeper.

"I meant paracetamol. I'm well aware that you don't want me touching you."

Turning away, she stalked from the living room, leaving him still trying to reach for words.

Leaning his head back into the plush chair, he cursed himself.

Rubbing his still aching head, he looked at her home. Her cottage must be at least two hundred years old, and the Victorian sash window faced straight out onto the quiet High Street. A plain white net curtain kept prying eyes out, and let light in. Although not much light. The clouds had only cleared to reveal the late autumn sun for a brief time. But as they approached late afternoon and the setting sun, the grey had taken hold. Shadows spread across the floor, and the comfort of her home enveloped him. His breaths became deep and easy, as his eyes drifted shut.

It was her scent that reached him first; a warm day on a calm sea. He smiled slowly as the warm glow of the sun touched his closed eyes, and the softness of her hand laid on his shoulder. Her voice husky as she whispered his name.

Slowly opening his eyes, the light created shafts, glimmering. Her eyes were so blue, as she looked down at him, the sunlight directly behind her. She said his name again, and he reached up, to run his finger along the smooth line of her jaw, easing his palm under the heavy sweep of her hair, to cup her cheek. "Ellie."

His voice was rough, he didn't know why. But her skin was warm and petal soft. Her hair brushed his forearm as he stared up at her, her pupils expanding, almost eclipsing the blue.

Her warm breath touched him as her lips parted, and he found he couldn't take his eyes from them. They looked inviting, beautifully curved and full. And seeming to answer his thoughts, with a whispered "oh," she brought their lips together.

Shifting his fingers through the silky strands, he gripped the back of her head, pulling her closer.

Groaning as she tipped her head, sweeping her tongue across his lips, he met her tongue with his own. Loving the rich, dark taste of her.

The weight of her, leaning into his chest made him feel strong, made him feel... needed? He couldn't question what arced through his brain, as the feel of her in his embrace overtook everything else.

Her breath rushed out as he kissed her jaw, the line of neck, but with a sudden gasp, she jerked back.

Nearly stumbling as she came to her feet, she pushed her hands into the pockets of her jeans.

Red flags of colour lit her cheekbones, and her eyes, surrounded by dark, thick lashes looked sleepy and sinful.

Taking another step away from him, he realised there was no sun behind her. But a side-lamp that she must've turned on. Had he drifted off?

"You've been asleep for nearly an hour." Gesturing, hesitantly at the side table, she'd put a glass of water and two paracetamol beside him. "And you won't sleep tonight, if you sleep now..."

Her words trailed off as she looked awkwardly away. Her lips red from the pressure of his.

"An hour?!"

She shrugged, "I thought you could do with the rest. Did it help?"

His body felt like it'd been super-charged. But he was pretty sure that was from kissing her, although his mind was quieter than it had been in a good number of months. "I think it did, thank you."

He swallowed the pills, took a gulp of water, giving himself a minute or two to orientate himself.

"Do we have to worry about a magical-working here? I told you Thea's ontop of things."

Reaching into his pocket, he took out a palm-sized disc of aquamarine, holding it flat in his hand and lifting it to shoulder height.

"Magic has been cast here.
Tell me what for.
Reveal its aims.
So I can be sure."

The crystal disc hummed, as power trilled through the house.

Adam watch Ellie smile slightly as laughter tinkled all around them, and soft taps sounded at the windows. Echoing whispers floated on the air, as the aquamarine warmed in his palm.

"Love resides here,
And happiness abundant.
This home is watched over,
By witches of old."

Offering thanks he wrapped the crystal in his grasp, breaking the connection. Before sliding it back into his pocket.

Ellie had gone to the bookcase. She turned back with a

small porcelain dish and a tin, he raised a brow at her when she handed them to him.

"Mint humbugs, we keep them all over the place, the spirits love them."

Popping the lid off the tin, he saw it was indeed full of mint humbugs, and couldn't stifle a laugh. "Humbugs? You all leave humbugs?"

Merely rolling her eyes at him, she took a handful from the tin, put them in the dish, and leant over the sofa, leaving them on the window ledge. "Thank you." She gave the window a little tap, before turning back around. "Don't you leave something in thanks when you ask for help?"

"Sure." Shaking his head, he repeated himself, "Sure. Of course. But I tend to put out a kind of all-purpose offering, at set times of the year."

"Uh-huh." Sitting back on the sofa, she clasped her hands between her knees. "Anyway, you heard what she said: my home is watched over, so I'll take you home."

"I'm not going anywhere, Ellie." Giving her a firm nod, as her jaw dropped, he raised his hand. "I mean it. Jason was right. This house is *watched over* not protected. And I'm zapped after the last twenty four hours, I won't be able to work that kind of spell for—I don't know—twelve hours, or at least something to eat and good night's rest. You, and I, have learnt some serious shi... stuff," he stumbled, not sure why he was correcting himself, "in the last few hours. And you know knowledge is a magical signature, leaving you open. Jess is MIA and Jason is hunting something I'd hoped never existed. We're safer together; the cloaking and protection I lay on myself will extend to wherever I am, and where I am is staying near you, until I can be sure for myself that you're properly protected. I got you into this, and I'll make sure you're safe."

She closed her mouth, and opened it again. Before finally

shutting it and leaving the room. He just caught her mutter through gritted teeth.

"I suppose I'll make up the spare room for you then."

He grinned as her perfectly round backside sashayed away from him.

He could feel the energy from her temper buzzing around him as he rummaged through her kitchen cupboards. He could detect, as opposed to hear, the sharp snap of the duvet as she snapped it back, and her huffy mumbling to herself as she moved around upstairs.

Her snit left him with a little smile. He'd got under her skin, after all the years of her being under his, the tide was turning.

Her cupboards were painfully bare: some potatoes, a cucumber, two bottles of red wine and what looked like a frozen chilli that felt distinctly like it had come from Thea. Opening the two drawers in her under-the-counter fridge, he found half a block of cheese. "Limited options..."

Turning full circle, he scanned the sides. "And no microwave."

Popping the frozen square of chilli out of the plastic container, it clattered into a saucepan, and holding his hand over the top he brought heat to his palm, melting the frost away, before putting it over a low heat on the hob.

Doing the same with the large potatoes, he cooked them through before putting them in the oven.

He'd grated cheese and was pouring wine by the time she came back downstairs, stopping in the doorway. She'd twisted her hair into a hasty bun, and pinned it on top of her head, and taken off her hoodie, leaving her in a black t-shirt with the Stoney Bay logo on.

"It smells... good in here." The hesitation in her words had him smiling.

"Well, I didn't have much to work with."

She shrugged nonchalantly. Holding a grey t-shirt towards him. "I don't cook much. Here, it's Marc's, you can't keep walking around in that." She looked pointedly at his charred t-shirt. "And I'm assuming you'll want a bath, not a shower?"

Looking down at himself, the once-white top was burnt and fraying in patches, the hem not meeting his cargo shorts in places. "What a twenty four hours, huh?" Grabbing the remaining hem he pulled it off, taking the grey one from her and putting it on. "I still can't believe Jason is a wolf."

Picking up the two glasses of wine, he placed them at the table, and pulled out a chair. "Ellie?"

She seemed to have frozen in the doorway, before shaking her head and stepping into the kitchen. She threw the balled up shirt in the bin, before sitting with him, taking a healthy sip of wine.

"I'd always figured there was something other about him. Because he, kind of... well, *seethes*, if you know what I mean?" She rested her jaw in her palm, and her elbow on the table as he spoke.

"I suppose." He thought back to the intense teenager he remembered Jason being, if he'd've known more, he would've seen it. But then, wasn't hindsight a wonderful thing? "I've only been with him, in the flesh, a few times in the last few years. Otherwise it was FaceTime, or whatever, if he was with Jess. So I didn't pick up on it."

Taking another sip, Ellie nodded, "and you were busy convincing yourself that Jess had a nice *normal* life, so you weren't looking for it."

"I..." Ready to fire back something short and undoubtedly ugly, he swallowed the words, and the dark look. "Probably." He released a sigh, and shifted around, propping his bound leg up on the chair in front of him. "I'm knackered, I want to eat and sleep, in that order. But I need to put some things straight in my mind." Her blue eyes were cautiously wide as he held her gaze, her hair and the girlie cut of her t-shirt making her look so much younger than the twenty six years he knew her to be. Still the pretty young thing from years ago. "What has been going on for them to block me out?"

Setting down her glass with a bump, her teeth, once again, worried her bottom lip, drawing his eyes. She'd be no good at poker.

"Adam." She rubbed her palms together, clearly looking for the right words. "Thea and Jess have both tried to talk to you about this over the years. It's not my place," she waved her hands on either side of her, "to stand between you and your sisters. You have to go to them."

Disagreeing even though he knew she was right, he frowned into his wine. She was right, dammit. But he needed something to try and get things straight in his mind... "Okay... so what *will* you tell me?"

Coming to her feet, she stepped to the oven, crouching down to check the potatoes, and stir the contents of the pan.

Turning to face him, she leant back against the side, the black sky framing her through the large window.

"Anything I say now will have to go back to where it started, and you'll end up yelling and I can't be arsed to deal with your temper."

Shocked by her bluntness, he couldn't help a sharp bark of laughter. "Straight from the hip. Tell it like it is, why don't you, Ells."

Shaking her head, she reached for her wine, and settled back to her comfortable lean. "I mean it. You think one sort-of decent day of communication between us puts the past to bed, and it doesn't. You don't know the half of what goes on around here, and I'm not at liberty to share. I can tell you what *I've* seen, and what *I've* dealt with. But I guarantee it'll send you back to banging your drum about how all this is my fault, blah blah. Not to mention,"—she was really on a roll now, the sharp look she angled his way telling him not to risk her annoyance further—" the fact that this 'sort-of decent day' has involved you *needing* help, Jess going missing, us finding out that vampires are real, and coming face to face with a bloody WEREWOLF! So I don't think this qualifies as remotely normal—do you?!" Her voice had risen, as she'd run through the day's events, and his awkward grimace of agreement as he searched for a way to explain, wasn't helping.

Holding his hands up in surrender, he nodded, "I know, I do. It's been a strange—I don't even know what to call it—day? But I'm trying to tell you that I get it. Finally. It's taken me seven years, I grant you."

His words were rich with emotion, as he all but beseeched her to listen. "But I get it; there's no blame to lay at anyone's door, and the magic woke up for a reason, and I've been an arse to you, and my sisters, apparently. But other things are out there, and Jess and Thea, and you, need to know a new set of rules now. Living with a foot in the everyday, and a foot in the magical plain means there are precautions that have to be taken, and new risks. And I have to explain—"

"You still don't get it do you? You *still* think you're the protector. The one who has to sweep in and sort everything out." Her hands sat on her hips as she shook her head, her brows raised as she looked up at the ceiling. "Gods, Adam. I know I'm not breaking any kind of trust to Jess by spelling this one out for you; what do you think Jess and Jason do? You saw their office, can you imagine how many *other* creatures Jess comes into contact with?! You know her magical base is psychometry, she knows more about the magical past than probably anyone!"

Going wholly still, he felt her words like a sharp wind. One of many today. He had let them all down, so completely. "I didn't know that. I didn't know she had a base power. What's Thea's?"

His voice sounded so totally defeated, even to his own ears. And she'd mistakenly betrayed a trust. What a mess they were making.

"Ellie, tell me, what difference does it make now?" He gentled his voice as he spoke.

She moved around the kitchen, laying out plates, busying herself with dishing dinner. So much so, that he didn't think she would answer.

"Divination, Thea's base power is reading people; the future, the past, it doesn't matter. But Jess reads objects; buildings, relics, but always in the past. We always figured that if you ever decided to use your magic, yours would somehow be based around the present."

She kept her back to him as she continued to speak. "Thea's magic is strong, especially in the last couple of years. She can also move from one place to the other, she says that its *teleporting*."

He heard the smile in her voice, and knew he'd missed some inside joke... something else that he'd missed.

"Unlike when you *haze*, it doesn't seem to tax her as much. Her spell casting is powerful too."

This he knew, at least he had that much. "She told me about the spell casting."

Ellie carried the plates to the table, lifting surprised eyes to his. "She did?"

He could sense the weight of her guilt at revealing his sisters secrets. He could at least ease that where he was able. He nodded. "When I got back from Greece. She said that she'd been doing a lot of studying to learn how to stop her empathy from constantly allowing others to drain her, and the side effect had been learning how to spell cast."

Pushing her dinner around her plate, Ellie nodded. "And I suppose you thought that meant she was just putting up barriers to keep others out so she could live a nice, normal, safe, little life?"

It all sounded so painfully patronising to him now, like he really had been patting them on the head while he did 'important' things. How much bigger of a wanker was he going to feel by the time this was over?

"I sound like a total knob."

Ellie chuckled around a mouthful of food, her smile warming her eyes as she looked at him. "You do seem to have your moments."

CHAPTER 6

CLICKING THE BEDROOM DOOR SHUT, he left the light off.

Plugging his phone in to charge, he crossed to the bed, pulling back the crisp white duvet.

Untucking the towel at his hips, he dropped it over the footboard, and sank onto the mattress, letting the cool sheets chill his skin. He'd bathed awkwardly in her tub, with his booted leg dangling over the side.

He'd let the bath run deliberately hot, steam filling the bathroom. With so many thoughts filling his head they seemed to mill about with the vapours.

He'd let his sisters down. He'd been so convinced he needed to keep them protected, keep them away from this life. If he was brutally, painfully honest, he'd even let doubt convince him they wouldn't have coped...

He cringed at the admittance, knowing they would skin him alive when he told them. And he had to tell them.

He would admit everything, explain everything. And even though he knew at the end they would love him anyway, he deserved to eat his serving of humble pie.

Dropping back onto the pillows, he pulled the duvet over his naked body.

The walls were white, like the sheets. The woodwork, the ornate French desk and chair, all white. The grey rug on the limed wood floor was like everything else in her house; neat as a pin. The rug perfectly square, like it daren't move.

Her home wasn't anything like he would've thought. It reminded him of winter mornings in the bay; glassy grey ocean, against a dove coloured sky. Still fog and the kind of quiet the soul yearned for.

He knew her garden was kept from the ocean by a tall flint wall, and he wondered what she grew there.

He'd glimpsed her bedroom, the door slightly ajar while she'd turned off lights downstairs.

A large piece of rough blue calcite sat on the delicate bedside table. The ornate, white bedstead took up most of the room, and an oil painting of a moonlit seascape hung above the bed.

The essence of her was so strong, it had called to him, the rhythmic lulling of an endless sea, as ever drawing him in. It was only the sound of her approaching the stairs that had sent him guiltily on, like he'd been caught in the act.

Moving fully into the centre of the bed, he let his arms drop wide. The large Victorian sash stared out into the night, she hadn't bothered to dress the first floor windows.

The star and moonlit sky peered in at him, as the full Hunter Moon rose higher. The night teemed with energy; trepidation and fulfilment. This cycle was one of personal power, this full moon was a completion—all full moons were—but this Hunter Moon was heavier than most, it was about the self, a realisation of one's true being.

He'd been shown a harsh and unforgiving image, he'd barely been able to stomach his own reflection as he'd bathed.

The tall mirror had stared uncompassionately back at him, forcing him to turn away in disgust.

But now, he lay here, with the night pulsing, sending warnings that he was sure weren't meant for him, and he had no way to decipher them. He didn't want to dream, didn't want to be left in the cold dark ocean, while those who meant the most to him left him behind.

But sleep crept up on him, thick and fast, sinking its claws in and pulling him under. Pain and rage tore at him, fear and uncertainty, wrapped in a blackness he couldn't drag himself out of. Fur and fangs under the bright, full moon.

Until finally he surfaced into vivid dream-state, breathing heavy, sweat making his skin tacky as he leant against the heavy oak door of Jess and Jason's office.

His feet were bare, his leg free of confinement, and his hand curled around the iron handle.

The door swung widely, the skirting and coving seeming to undulate as he stepped inside, as if The Fates were bending to allow him admittance—to allow him to see.

But Jess wasn't here. No-one was. The fire was lit, as it had been earlier and the lights glowed, low and distant.

He paced across the room, the now-thin Victorian rug hard beneath his feet, as he walked towards the large notice board he'd seen before.

Photos and drawings littered the board; the Stone of Scone, the Sword of Mercy, the club of Dagda, the Cintamani Stone—knowledge battered him as his glance flittered from image to image. Some had been found and hidden, or returned. Some, were still missing.

And there, pinned in amongst what could only be determined as the slush pile, was a hand-drawn image of three blue apothecary bottles on yellowing paper. The complete picture hidden behind the post-it note stuck to it.

The handwriting on the post-it was hardly visible; like a

whisper in a crowded room. Two ticks, followed by one question mark.

His hand reached out, shaking at the force of will it took to grip the note, peeling it away.

The first two bottles stood tall and proud, the other lay on its side, the blue of the glass more murky, the corked stopper pushed impossibly far into the neck. Looking like it would never come out.

Jerking awake, he bolted upright.

Alone in the ocean or this?

Looking down. The picture, the note, weren't in his grasp. Beads of sweat pricked from his skin, the chill air dragged her nails across him.

His body shivered as he fought to calm his breath. He stared out at the ashen morning light, before glowering down at his empty hands, his remembered dream. One of the bottles had been destroyed, he knew it. It had been lying down, dirty and faded. The cork wedged tight. Telling him, surely, that he'd no longer be able find it. What was the point in searching for the other two now?

Defeat rattled through him. Rage and dread, bitterness and wild confusion. He'd wanted the bottles so his sisters could give their magic back. Hadn't he? Wasn't this what it'd all been about?

But now Jess's, and seemingly Thea's, life was steeped in magic, they needed to keep it to stay safe. So he didn't need the bottles anymore...

Don't you?

The whisper was tender. A kindness that comforted his stretched nerves.

Had this really been only about Thea, only about Jess?

Somewhere in amongst all this, he'd convinced himself that they'd all be better off without magic, without the pain and the agony. But he'd come home this summer, and they'd laughed about their magic, joked about it. The relief that they weren't suffering as he was had been consuming.

The only thing outweighing the relief had been the confusion. Why was he suffering, what was wrong with him?

He's anger at Ellie had always been tied to his assumption that his sisters were suffering in some form as well. But now he knew it was only him. Why?

Every day since he'd been dragged through the Mediterranean and thrown back onto the deck of the *Miss Julia,* with his leg busted and broken, it had been one blow after another. Everything he thought he knew, thought he fought for, had been torn away. Until he was left with the stark truth.

He wanted rid of the magic. *He* was tired of hurting, *he* was tired of not being in the bay, not being with his family, not living the life here that he'd always wanted to; repairing boats, watching the seasons. *Coming home to the arms of a good woman, a loving family.*

The whisper stilled him, as Ellie flashed before his eyes, laughing. Murphy lay in front of the fire. Ellie's ladylike hand wrapped in his.

Magic had taken it all. Years had gone by. And what did he have to show for it except a rage that became more uncontrollable with each passing month?

Fire pooled in his belly, heating his skin, and he pleaded with the weakness of his own anger. *Don't let it win, don't let it rise.*

The chant rolled through his mind, and the energy charge filled the room, feeding the fire that lived within him.

Until the bedroom door abruptly thrust open.

The softly-lit hallway threw rays around her, creating shadows across the floor. Her hair hung loose across her smooth shoulders, her full breasts rose with her sharp intake of breath.

"Ellie don't..." His voiced cracked as he said her name, lifting his hand towards her, warning her off.

The fiery embers that traced the veins of his forearms and filled his palms didn't stop her from rushing to him. The bedroom door swinging shut behind her.

Winter morning light bathed her as she knelt on the bed. The plain cotton vest top and shorts revealed her sun kissed skin; softly curved thighs, delicate wrists. Lushly flared hips and small waist.

Lust warred with rage as her misty-morning scent reached him. His nostrils flared as he sucked it in, filling his lungs with her.

Oblivious to the danger she reached out, cupping his elbows, lifting his arms, tracing her thumbs along the lava burning hotly through his skin.

Her palms and fingers took the weight, sliding down his arms towards his wrists.

As if still trapped in the dream, he stared in a trance-like state as midnight and stars pooled in her hands. It felt as if she carried the tide in her fingertips.

The burning calmed, as if releasing a sigh of peace, dissipating beneath her touch. Power—magic, wondrous and pure —reverberated through him, and he couldn't hold back the gruff moan at how right everything felt in that one, astonishing moment.

Shocked blue eyes darted up to his, and he was sure he could see the caps of the waves and the roll of the tide reflected there.

Her lips had delicately parted, and he wanted her gentleness, her purity.

Her tenderness called to him, and the fire that lived within him. She, like no other woman, called to the creature within.

His eyes glowed with the light of golden galaxies as he held her, trapped with his gaze.

She waited for his rage to spill out; she'd halted the burning—unasked. She wasn't nineteen, now she knew better. She knew *him* better. But no matter the consequence she'd bear it. If the alternative was watching him burn, as he had on the beach, she had no other choice.

Her hands had glowed with power, like they had last night when she'd kissed him.

Her breath lodged in her throat as she waited, she knew he wouldn't physically hurt her. But to go back to the icy hatred had tears scalding her eyes.

They'd almost moved on.

His chest rose and fell with the heaviness of his breaths, and the thick silence seemed to breathe with him.

Releasing his wrists, she slowly lifted her hands, as one would when slowly backing away from a wild tiger.

Kneeling up, she made to ease off the bed, when he moved.

His large, capable hands encircled her waist, halting her as she was, looking ever-so-slightly down at him.

His hair was more auburn in the winter morning light. His impossibly broad shoulders, and the expanse of skin and muscle on display made her palms itch to touch him. Made her heart race, and heat pool in her belly.

His hands were hot through the cotton, and she wanted to arch into his touch, rub herself against him. Revel in him.

The slightest lift at the corner of his mouth gave him a feral expression, the glint that lit his eyes might've frightened her if she wasn't so turned on.

He took her weight easily, lifting her the few scant centimetres from the bed to bring her closer, closing the gap between them, fitting her body to his.

Her cool thighs pressed against his hot stomach, the

sizzling heat of him driving away the chill, as his arms wrapped around her hips, locking her to him.

Her breasts rested just beneath his jaw as he pressed his face to her, scraping his stubbled cheek across her collarbone, making her breath catch and sending a shiver down her spine.

Finally releasing her pent up breath, she laid her cheek on his head, touching his shoulders, his back, holding him, breathing him in.

"Gods', Ellie. I want you, I'm so fucking tired of fighting it." His husky murmur sank into her, and she moaned in agreement.

His fingers slid up her neck, into her hair, angling her to look at him.

"Stay with me, Ellie. Please." The words were barely audible, his eyes glowed, a fiery warmth in the insipid light. Her only response was to meet his lips with hers.

There was no careful exploration, it was frenzied.

Panting and raw, a carnal battle. She gripped his jaw, feasting on his mouth, their breaths sounding loud in the silence.

She could feel his fingers digging into her hips as he arched his neck to meet her kiss.

She wanted it all; to touch all of him, to see all of him. His skin was hot and smooth beneath her palms, his back and shoulders corded with muscle.

His lips were hungry, he tasted of autumn and dark starry nights, and she released a small whimper at the throbbing ache only he could cure.

Sod the consequences, she needed him. Had always yearned for *him*. The spark he'd fanned to life years ago with just a look was ready to burn.

His hands touched the bare skin of her waist and she gasped at the heat, at the little shocks bouncing between them.

He dragged her down to the bed, laying over her. His eyes glowed, and she was stunned at his beauty. The strong line of his nose, the hard angle of his jaw.

Her hair fanned as he rolled her beneath him. The white sheets the perfect backdrop. Her lush little frame was nipped at the waist. Full hips and breasts, dainty hands and softly curved thighs had blood pounding away from his brain. She was a beauty, dazzling like the summer sun.

Wide blue eyes, heavy with desire, slowly blinked as she lifted her palms to his chest, stroking the ridges of muscle. Her teeth caught her bottom lip as she watched her fingers brush his skin.

He froze, watching her pink tongue lick her lips as she reached his ribs, sliding warm, smooth palms over his hips to cup his buttocks.

Giving him a squeeze, she widened her thighs, pulling him more snugly to her.

And he groaned, low and long. The thin cotton couldn't hide how hot, the luscious core of her was.

"Ellie..." His voice broke as he circled his hips. Her fingers gripping his cheeks tightened, urging him, along with her sweet gasp, to do it again.

Holding heavy and still against her, he cupped her cheek, laying his forehead to hers, squeezing his eyes shut for a second.

"I gotta get a grip, or I'll just slide into your sweet heat, and this will all be over. I don't want to hurry, Baby."

Her lips traced his jaw, his cheek, as he spoke. The summer scent of her filling his senses. Her hips tried to lift into him, despite how heavily he'd pinned her to the bed, and he groaned as her hands touched wherever she could reach.

Frustration filled her gaze as it locked with his.

"We'll go slow next time, Adam, just fill me. Please..."

The whispered plea was enough. Logical thought fled as

he got hold of the waistband of her shorts, ready to push them off.

Magic and energy filled the room, as the gold and purple orb materialised above them. Stilling them both.

The globe disintegrated, showering them with the glowing sparks as a whisper, carried on a cool breeze, passed over them.

She is here. She is home.

Ellie stared up at him. Dark lashes prettily framed her large, blue wide-set eyes, as uncertainty and what looked like embarrassment chased desire and wanton-abandon away.

"She has always been the queen of lousy timing..." He tried to smile down at her, but his damn body ached. Unsatisfied need burned in his gut, and he wanted nothing more than sink into her, wiping that worried frown away.

But she was already moving, and he had no option but to free her as she hurried out from underneath him, coming to her feet beside the bed.

"Adam—I'll..." She stopped, and took a short breath, deliberately putting her arms firmly by her sides. "I'll get dressed and take you over." Turning away she made to leave, but once again stopped, her hand on the doorknob. "Your dream, or pain or whatever it was, woke me. That's why I came in without knocking. I didn't come in for..." she gestured between them, "this."

Before he could clear his mind enough to respond she was gone. Closing the bedroom door quietly behind her.

"Fuck it." Scraping his hands through his hair, he cursed Jess, and as he stared down at his booted leg, he cursed that too.

She was the brightness in amongst all this. And he was tired of living in shadow.

Standing at the top of the stairs, he concluded that wasting magic to haze down would be foolhardy, as gods' knew what help Jess might need. Trying to get down this narrow flight would also, most likely, see him pitch arse-over-tit and bugger himself up even more.

Heaving a huge sigh, he kept everything crossed that she stayed in the kitchen, as he sat on the top-step, and began to shuffle down on his bum.

"Of all the fucking indignity." He barely finished muttering as she came into the hallway, already calling his name.

"Adam? Are you alrigh...?" Lowering her gaze, she went quiet.

"Go-on laugh it up. I'm well aware I look like a total git."

She was clearly doing her best to suppress the smile. But her lips twitched with the effort. Lightly clearing her throat, she raised her brows, humour dancing in her eyes. "Not at all, however you need to get about is fine by me."

Getting close enough to the bottom, he rose to his feet, feeling much more comfortable to be head and shoulders above her delicate five foot four frame. "Sod off."

Stifling a chuckle, she walked round him to the front door. "Come on, let's get you to Jess."

He trailed after her to the car. She obviously thought she was dropping him off and running out on him. He pursed his lips. *Not gonna happen.*

Pulling up outside Jess's cottage, it looked much the same as it had the night before; car on the drive, the front windows shadowed. But as they stopped outside, Adam couldn't shake the niggling thought that she'd been here all along.

They'd most definitely be having words...

The low sound of the engine idling had Adam turning away from the house to look at Ellie.

Her brows raised in question. "Will you be okay getting to the front door?"

He pursed his lips, folding his arms across his chest. She

really was determined to get rid of him. "We're both going in, Ellie."

The deep green V-neck she was wearing looked as soft as her skin. It hung loosely to one side, revealing a smooth expanse of collarbone. She'd scooped her hair into what looked like an incredibly complicated twist, showing the elegant curve of her neck. And the V of the sweater sat perfectly on the swell of her breasts. The dark blue jeans moulded her hips and arse, which had given him pause as they'd walked to the car. His mouth had dried as she'd bent, and slid into the bucket seat.

He'd been wearing t-shirts and the same half a dozen pairs of cargo shorts on rotation since he'd broken his leg. Occasionally throwing a hoodie over the top.

Exciting.

He ignored his little voice laughing at him. It wasn't like he wanted to *dress up* for her. But she was fresh as a daisy; buttery looking brown leather flats, perfume, earrings that sparkled... she looked classically pretty. And he felt... flat. Like he'd been sleeping in the woods for weeks.

He wanted a hot shower, clean jeans, a nice shirt.

He wanted to be rid of this bloody boot!

A couple of surgeries, pins and plaster, before coming back to the U.K. More x-rays, more being poked and prodded.

He was doing everything he was told, but he knew, deep down, that it was going to take more than conventional medicine. He was almost sure the bone had healed, but the constant ache and weakness, he feared came from the magic, or the poison, of whatever had attacked him.

"This is between you and Jess, it'll be a good chance for you two to talk, and you don't need me in the way."

Her voice was calm, her words sounded practiced.

"Sorry, Ells, not happening. I need to lay a protection spell on you and your home, and we both need to know if Jess's trouble is still looking for her."

She gripped the wheel, and took a calming breath before speaking. "Look, I've already said I'm okay with you putting the protection on me and my home. You don't have to be with me to do it, and whatever *it* is, is looking for Jess, not me. And if *it* is a vampire, then Jason's looking for her, and she'd do better to be getting as far away from him as possible."

"Don't be stubborn, Ellie, my sisters are going to lynch me for endangering you as it is. And any magical working is stronger when done at source, you know that."

The knock on his passenger window had them both jumping.

Jess opened the door with a grin. "Are you two going to sit in the car and argue, or are you coming in?"

She looked okay, better than okay. She looked relaxed and happy, and not at all like she'd been in the midst of a blood bath two days ago.

"And it's bloody nice to see you too." Pulling himself out from the car, he wrapped her in a tight hug. He was struck with scents of home and childhood, and couldn't believe the emotion that welled up within him. Stepping back, he grasped her shoulders, catching her gaze. "Are you okay?"

Magic thrummed through her, it buzzed in his grip, stronger than he'd detected before.

Her brown eyes sparkled with joy. "I'm good. Honestly. Come on, come indoors."

Stepping out of the car, Ellie shut the door. Surprised to find him waiting for her.

His hand settled warmly on her lower back as they followed Jess down the path, and she couldn't decide whether to shake him off or lean into him.

The fire was happily burning in the hearth, and Ellie was

struck by the sheer force of joyful energy that teemed through Jess's lovely home.

Turning towards the open-plan kitchen Ellie came face-to-face with one of the most handsome men she'd ever seen. His caramel-coloured hair and sultry brown eyes, were set off by a straight nose and killer cheekbones. He was obviously tall and fabulously well put together. There was also something familiar about his aura that Ellie couldn't quite put her finger on...

"Hey, I'm Sebastian... Seb."

She took his hand, his warm, rough grip firmly shook. And wasn't surprised to detect that same seething energy she'd only felt from one other person.

"I'm Ellie." Turning slowly, sure in the knowledge that Adam was going to go into full-on 'big brother' mode, she smiled reassuringly at him. "And this is Adam..."

"Jess's brother." Another firm shake, accompanied by a suspiciously long look from Adam, left Seb battling to hide a slight smile.

"Good to meet you."

Jess whirled into the kitchen, clicked on the kettle and took cups from the cupboard. "Oh Adam, that's enough of that." She planted her palms on the breakfast bar, staring at him across it, and gave him a sharp look. "Now then, would you like to tell me again how you *don't use magic*, and yet you still managed to leave that little seeing-eye-orb to spy on me?"

Ellie eased quietly back, perching on the edge of the wide window board, waiting to see how Adam was going to handle this one. She knew well enough that both sisters had just been waiting for a chance to catch Adam at magic.

Continuing on with a wave of her hand, Jess flicked her long dark hair back across her shoulder. "And I feel I should add that a *very* good friend of mine, might've mentioned that you just happened to turn up at the museum." Nodding at Ellie, Jess's stare became even more frosty. "Having dragged Ellie up there too." Her slim, dark brows arched haughtily as she waited for her brother's response.

Seb swung casually off the bar stool, and came to sit next to Ellie on the window ledge, giving her a conspiratorial smirk. "I'm staying out of the way for this one."

Chuckling in agreement, she crossed her arms, as he did the same.

Adam glared sharply at the pair of them as Jess spoke, "Jess, be careful what you say in front of..." His words trailed off as he gestured towards Seb, and Ellie cringed, wanting to put her head in her hands at his rookie move.

"You don't need to worry about Seb, he has a

far better idea of what goes on in this family than you do. As does Jason, for that matter, What the bloody-hell were you thinking, tearing up to London in the middle of the night! You both could've been hurt!"

Adam was starting to look like a berated child, as he cautiously slid onto a barstool.

"I wasn't thinking ab—"

"You're damn right you weren't. You know, it's about bloody time you realised that Thea and I can take care of ourselves." Jess was really working up a good head of steam now. "And I am going to get really angry about this, just so you know. But you're going to have to wait for that pleasure; I've called Thea."

At Adam's shocked expression, Ellie covered her mouth with her hand to hide her grin. Everything was going to be okay, Adam had shown his magical hand, so to speak, and Jess wasn't going to let it go. Ellie let the wave of relief sweep through her. It wasn't going to have to be her that started the hard conversation of what was between them all, it was going to take care of itself.

"You called Thea?"

Ellie found herself feeling sorry for him, as he looked at Jess, his mouth slightly open.

"I did, this morning, after I found your little spy-device. She's coming home early; day after tomorrow, and we're going to talk about this, Adam. All of it. So you'd better be feeling chatty."

She planted her hands on her hips, lavender sparks firing in her eyes as she glared at her brother. "And I'd like it if you can be here too, Ellie?"

Ellie nodded. "Of course, it's long overdue."

At her words, Jess seemed to calm, and she rushed across the room to hug her.

Surprised, Ellie hugged her back. "What's all this?"

Giving her an extra squeeze, Jess pulled back. "I'm just glad you're okay, and that my stupid brother didn't get you into any trouble."

Turning on the stool, Adam faced them. "I know I've screwed up. I haven't left Ellie alone since, I just need to put some protection on her and—"

"Oh good grief." Jess rolled her eyes in his general direction. "Ellie, have you got the charm Thea made for you?"

Placing her palm to her chest, she grasped the long gold necklace, pulling it from beneath her jumper. The sunstone and moonstone charm hung as the pendant. "Of course, I take it off to sleep, but otherwise—"

"Well not anymore, you wear it all the time." Reaching inside the collar of her silky blouse, Jess pulled out a similar charm, on a long chain. "Thea gave me mine when I bought Adam back from Greece." Raising a brow in Adam's direction, before turning back to Ellie, she said, "I think we both knew he was up to something. It's for protection and balance, and it will completely cloak you from anything... let's say, unfriendly."

"Like a vampire?" Adam's tone held more than a little edge.

"Well, Jason's taking the lead on that." Jess unconsciously reached for Seb's hand, and Ellie didn't miss Adam noticing.

"Oh. And that's another bloody thing! Jess, why didn't you tell me Jason was a *wolf*?" He whispered the last word, glaring sharply at Seb when he laughed.

Seb cupped the back of Jess's nape as he raised his brows at Adam, his grin devilish. "Is that a problem?" His eyes wavered from their friendly brown, a bright iridescent blue eclipsing the iris as he spoke.

Leaning his elbow on the breakfast bar, Adam rubbed his forehead. "Well of course, that's just perfect."

Taking pity on her brother, Jess released Seb's hand and went to him. "Are you okay? Jason said you seemed quite... shocked, to see him in wolf form. Have you never seen one before?"

Ellie watched them, Jess so dark, almost gothic. Adam more like a California surfer. He'd spent so long thinking he was protecting them, she knew it would do him good to realise they all had their strengths. But the rug really had been ripped out from under him.

"I *knew* they existed, have met one a few times. But at a pub you know, over a beer. Not in a dark museum, on all four paws, when I'm searching for my sister. He's a big bastard too."

Jess chuckled, hugging him. "I'll be sure to tell him that. It'll boost his ego." Releasing a huge sigh, she hugged him some more. "I'm so glad you're alright too, you idiot."

His brow creased, as he closed his eyes tight, and Ellie felt tears sting her eyes as she watched them.

As the moment passed, Jess stepped away, going back to the kitchen. "Right then, coffee?"

Knowing this was her moment, Ellie picked up her keys.

"No, thank you. I'm going to go, and let you all spend some time."

Adam's sharp 'no' had Jess raising her eyebrows, and Ellie inwardly cringed as he turned to her. "Don't leave, you said we need to sort this out."

Nodding, she gathered her thoughts, determined to get some time alone. "I did, and we will, but we're going to wait for Thea. And besides, I have a work meeting this afternoon." She checked her watch, "I've got a little time now to get my papers sorted. Just text me if you... if there's a problem." Wrapping her pendant in her palm, she held it for comfort. "And like Jess said, I'm perfectly safe now to go about my business—and I do have a business to go about."

Saying her goodbyes, she made fast work of getting out the door and driving off the island. She just needed some time, alone, to think. Or maybe not to think. Just time alone.

CHAPTER 7

"So, you and Ellie finally buried the hatchet then?"

After closing the front door behind Ellie, Jess had sauntered back to the kitchen, her left brow arched curiously as she spoke.

Adam lifted both brows at her, and glanced over at Seb. "Before you start digging into my life, I think you've got some explaining of your own to do, don't you?"

Giving him a coy smile, she held her palm out. "You'd like a formal introduction? Well, okay then. Adam, this is Sebastian Hunter, he's a historian at the Victoria and Albert Museum. He specialises in religious relics, and was at McGill University in Canada before Jason enticed him away. He's quite the genius, academically speaking." She threw Seb a wink. "He also happens to be a werewolf."

Adam watched the pair of them as she spoke, Seb squirmed beneath her praise, and rolled his eyes. It was clear the bond between them was strong, but still... "Is that how you and Jason know each other, are you related?"

Ellie was right, there was something *seething* about wolves.

Coming to his feet, Seb shook his head. "It would've been

easier, but no. I met Jason years ago, through work. I've only been a werewolf for a few months, apparently. But I've only been able to shift in the last few days"

The conversation was surreal, yet Adam couldn't help but warm to the guy. His aura and etheric field were clear, no dark spots. And it was clear he was head over heels for Jess.

He still had much explaining of his own to do, and was he learning so much about his sisters, that he couldn't very well get all big-brother-y, and risk shutting himself out of their lives. Again.

Bending and stretching his leg, he couldn't stifle the slightly delirious laugh, as he rubbed the back of his knee. "A few days huh? Christ-knows this has been the weirdest few days of my life. And that's bloody saying something. But I suppose you've had a pretty rough week. Let's hope we're through the worst of it."

"I'll drink to that." Seb patted his shoulder a he came over, and sat on the bar stool beside him. "Your leg playing up?"

"Just aching."

Jess came round to face him, her hands on her hips. "You've just been in the company of one of the best healers I know. Why, pray tell, haven't you let her heal you? You're obviously friends now." She put air quotes around the 'friends', and with one long look told him she didn't buy it for a minute.

Not wanting to get too deep into it without Thea, Adam tried to shrug it off. "It's complicated." At her huffed 'oh please,' he held both hands up in surrender. "Truly, there's more to it, and it just wouldn't be a good idea. Ellie knows it too."

On a sisterly sigh, she gave him an eye roll. "Well, can I at least give you a boost?"

"It would be gratefully received. Bloody thing is driving me nuts."

She began to rub her palms together, creating lilac sparks as magic gathered. "I'll have to start charging you a fee."

He laughed, the static of her power seeped into his aura as she continued the friction, warming her skin. "Fine by me. One bottle of Glen Scotia '92, coming your way."

Seb's murmured, "So that's your favourite," had Adam lifting his head in question.

"She said the Balvenie 30 was your choice, but didn't mention her own." Seb gave her a nod. "Nice."

As Jess stared at Seb, the energy running between them was so strong, that Adam was getting a charge from it, and her palms were arcing and crackling.

Clearing his throat he looked pointedly at her hands. "Jess, do you think you might want to get on with it?"

Her throaty chuckle made him smile, but the zap she gave his leg had him jerking in the chair. "Hey! Easy does it. Your bedside manner could do with some work, ya know." The tiny static shocks faded quickly, leaving the leg feeling virtually normal, and he came to his feet, enjoying being evenly balanced.

She gave him a poke in the arm as she finished. "Don't moan." Sending the last remaining sparks into the ether, she swept her hair over one shoulder, looking between the two men. "Seeing the time, I suppose you're both hungry?"

"I could eat."

"Sounds good to me."

Seb's agreement meshed with Adam's and he found himself liking him more.

"Could you run me home later, and take a detour past the pub so I can grab Murph?"

Despite the chill night, the boot encasing his left leg itched his overheated skin. He ignored the fact that the 'step, thump' of his gait made him sound like an approaching mass murderer in a horror movie, and he frowned down at Murphy's decidedly amused snort.

"Not helping, Buddy."

Murphy's toothy canine grin told Adam that Murphy didn't mind. And as they made their way slowly down the road to his house, Adam smoothed his soft head, grinning with him.

"But you gotta laugh, right? Besides, it's nice just to be able to take a walk in the fresh air without feeling like I'm going to fall on my face."

He'd had Jess and Seb drop him at the end of his road, so he and Murph could take the short walk home in the early evening air. The ocean was calm, the tide barely making a sound, and for the first time since Greece, he felt peaceful. If he really thought about it, he felt more calm and centred now than he had since the magic had first raced through him. He wasn't alone, there were things to discuss, that might even reveal the answers that he needed. He felt... hopeful.

He hadn't left any lights on when he'd gone to find Ellie. Two days seemed like a lifetime ago. But as they got closer he frowned to see the porch softly lit. The lamp in the living room shone through the shore facing window, and further into the house he could tell the kitchen light and the TV were on.

Murphy lifted his nose into the night air, catching every tell-tale scent. Adam waited for some kind of sign from Murph as to whether their visitor was friend or foe, when his tail lifted, and with a bark he raced ahead.

"Must be a friend then." Adam continued at his painstakingly slow pace. Frustrated anew by the boot and his stupid leg.

Woe betide whoever had come to see him, gods forbid they tried to cheer him up, or anything equally ridiculous.

Maybe it was Ellie.

The thought crept into his mind, and he brightened. Maybe she wanted to make sure he was okay?

He closed the open front door behind him, the sound of Murphy's paws on the wood kitchen floor reached him. Murph was prancing about like a puppy, being fussed over by a female voice with a very Irish accent.

Leaning against the doorjamb, he watched the light catch bright red hair, as Lucy O'Leary fussed over Murph.

He could feel the grin sliding over his face as she laughed, and turned in circles, while Murphy joined her, yipping and barking.

Finally coming to a stop, she smoothed his ears, touching her forehead to his, and Murphy closed his eyes in bliss.

"And it's good to see you too, Boyo."

The rhythmic lilt of her southern Irish brogue touched that bittersweet place in his soul, remembering how good things had been; the three of them together, Lucy, Dillon and him. She'd been a balm on the gaping wound that leaving his sisters had caused, and she'd become like a sister to him.

Rising to stand straight, her green eyes held that same mix of happy and sad he was sure his did. But her smile held something else. A grief that hadn't been there before.

"Luce?"

She slid her hands into the pockets of her snug-fitting jeans, her smile wobbled as a sheen of tears made her green eyes bright.

"It's Dillon. He's gone, Adam. He's gone." Her voice dried up, and one lone tear escaped her tight control, to roll down her cheek.

He wrapped her up, tight to him. Absorbing her tremors, or maybe they were his own?

He'd been so young when he'd sailed out of the bay,

shockingly powerful magic coursing through him. Rage and fear at what he was filling him.

Dillon had known instantly what he was. And Adam had found a friend. In those early days he couldn't imagine life without him.

How wrong he'd been.

The first waves of shock were numbing, as memories of the past flooded him. But as they stood, leaning on each other, old magic and the scents of Ireland encircled him. There was calm mixed with grief, telling him more clearly than she would that she'd made peace with her brother's death. But the slight fissions teasing the edges of her etheric field, warned that full balance had yet to be restored.

Catching her by the shoulders he looked down into her green eyes, as they swirled amber with emotion. "I can feel the need for punishment teeming all around you. We're going to be talking about that before you fly out of here on some mission of retribution."

A slight smirk tipped one side of her beautiful lips, and he wondered, not for the first time, why he couldn't have fallen for her. Why, even with all the years, with all the absences in-between, was Ellie the only female to fill his thoughts?

"The last thing I need is another brother telling me what I can, and cannot do." She poked him in the chest, giving him a zap at the same time, stepping from his embrace. "I still have two more brothers—who've already said the same thing, in case you were wondering. So knock it off."

Murphy pressed against her leg, lifting sad, sooty eyes, offering comfort.

Managing to flash Lucy a sharp glare, he smoothed Murphy's head as he passed, giving him a murmured 'good boy.'

He sat down, putting his hand behind his knee, to lift his booted leg onto another chair. He undid the velcro straps on the leg brace, groaning in bliss as the fresh air touched his hot, itchy skin.

The odd noise from Lucy had him opening his eyes to look up at her. To find her staring at his leg, brows raised, eyes wide, her hands pressed heavily to her stomach.

"Glory-be! Adam, what in the bloody-hell is that?"

He looked at his leg. "I suppose it is a bit gruesome." Pink scars riddled the skin, the muscle was awkward, slightly distorted from the second surgery. The broken bone, the pins, and a second fracture had made healing difficult and complicated. But it was the slight tinge to the skin that worried him. X-rays showed everything was healing—had virtually healed. But the leg wasn't getting any stronger. And couldn't take his weight without a magical boost.

"I don't care about gruesome. It looks fecking painful. It also looks like it bears a magical signature. Do you want some help with it?"

Hope raced through him, excitement flip-flopped in his belly at just the possibility of being rid of the boot. "You betcha! I didn't know you had magic from the healer cast. Fix me, woman!"

Her laughter was apologetic, as she patted his shoulder. "Me? No healer here, boyo. But you must have some decent Irish whiskey around this place to take the edge off, while I work a little disclosure spell to see what you're up against?"

Shaking his head at the wicked glint in her eye, he let his disappointed sigh fill the kitchen.

Pointing at the top cupboard, he waited for her to cross the room. "It's on the top shelf." He held a beat before adding, "Behind the proper scotch."

Snatching her hand back, she threw a "Ya fecker," over her shoulder, as she reached round the scotch like it would scald her, to get to the Connemara. "Heathen you are. You'll no longer be welcome at my house, drinking scotch whisky."

Sitting down, she poured a healthy three fingers for both of them. "But what I don't understand is, I know there's healers in the bay. From a strong line too, why are you struggling on?"

He held the first sip of whisky, let it warm his tongue before swallowing. "You remember how Dillon always said my magic never worked right. Like I was *missing* something?"

She rolled her eyes at that. "I do, yes. And like I always said, there was nothing *missing*, just more to come. It just took a bit of patience, didn't it?"

Here we go, time to start admitting the truth. To everyone.

"I didn't want to wait, so Dillon... I had him help it along."

Her chair legs scraping on the floor had Murphy lifting his head and his ears. "Oh for the love of Christ! What a stupid bloody thing to do." Her hair billowed and waved as she stalked across the kitchen. "And tell me, did it all go to plan?"

Sarcasm dripped from her voice, as she came to a standstill. The two inch heels on her ankle boots gave her slight frame a little extra height, not that she needed it. She'd always been a force to be reckoned with, and he'd just voluntarily put himself in her crosshairs.

You better talk fast, Lavelle.

He inwardly cursed his little voice; nothing he said was going to make it better.

"Of course it bloody didn't, Luce. As you can gather, I was twenty three, drunk and stupid." He knocked back the contents of the glass, before setting it down with a bang. "And it seemed like a good idea at the time."

"I have no words, Adam. I can't believe you both did something so stupid! I mean you," she gestured to all of him, with a dismissive wave of her hand, "didn't know much back then. But Dillon! Lord-alive, there's a price, he knows that. There must *always* be balance." Sitting back down with purpose, she clasped her hands on the table. "Now tell me exactly what you did."

Pinching the top of his nose, he braced himself for more shouting. "We didn't really work it out, we'd had a drink on the beach and he said he'd try and draw it up..."

She pursed her lips, her eyes barely a slit as she glared at him. "And..."

Pouring himself another scotch, and one for her—gods' knew she was going to need it—he took a breath. "I caught fire, and Dillon pushed me off the cliff into the ocean."

He knew he was done-for when her mouth simply hung-open, no shouting, no temper. Just complete disbelief.

"We were young, Luce. And stupid, like I said. And that's why I haven't asked Ellie or Marc to help me."

Furrowing her brow in confusion, she took a hefty swallow, hissing softly between her teeth as it went down. "This I've got to hear." Her voice was sickly-soft as she spoke. "And why, heavens knows, wouldn't you ask for a healing?"

He got a crawling sensation at the back of his neck, he'd always taken it as a warning sign; it was clearly a bit late. *How much more can you possibly fuck up?*

"It was Ellie that woke up the magic in the first place, and you remember how well I was doing after that?" His voice rose, as if shouting about it could make it all make sense. "Can you imagine if she'd actually finished?! And now, if I get the leg healed, who knows what else might *wake-up*. I can't deal with what I've got, let alone more."

He was panting, his leg throbbed and ached, and the skin was changing, colouring like one big, ugly, bruise.

"Hey now, hey now, calm down, boyo." She grabbed his hand, the old Irish magic thrumming from her, easing him. "What exactly did that to your leg?"

Just tell her all of it, get it all out.

"There are bottles, three." He panted as he spoke, talking

through the worst of the aching in his leg. "For me and my sisters. They come from when our magic was bound; I dreamed it. If I can gather all three bottles, then we don't have to have the magic anymore. I used a location spell, but I could only find one."

Murphy came to sit beside him, and he unconsciously smoothed his head.

"It was in an underwater cave, just off the island of Myrina. I went diving for it, but whatever lived in the cave had other ideas. It dragged me out, and I couldn't get back in. I blasted the entrance, which bounced me back, and whatever it was smacked the hell out of me, and deposited me back on the deck of the Miss Julia. The damage to my leg was pretty bad, so I called Jess. It should be healed by now, but it's not. So I'm staying in the bay until I can work it all out."

He turned the glass on the table, letting the light catch the crystal. "There, that's all of it."

"Adam Lavelle, that's the most open I've ever heard you be. It sounds like the abbreviated version, don't get me wrong. But boyo, I think you've been coming at this all to cock." She let go of his hand, patted it. "Why don't you ask your sisters if this is what they want?"

"I can't now. I've been so busy you see, *being Adam,* that I haven't understood that they're perfectly capable of taking care of themselves. And now Jess is mixed up with a wolf she'll be needing her magic."

Lucy went wholly still at his words, all colour washed from her face. "Your sister is seeing Jason?"

"You bloody knew! Of all the... does everyone keep me in the dark?!" He stared incredulously at her. "And no, not Jason. Seb."

A sinister light briefly lit her gaze, before she tapped it down, returning to the topic at hand. "It wasn't my place to say. And you deserved it, running around banging your chest, talking all the crap about how you 'know best' and 'keeping them safe.' I have brothers too don't I? I wasn't going to feed that fire. Besides, now it's all sorted, I can finally meet them. Unless you don't think that'd be a good idea?" Her smile was sweetly innocent, and he groaned at the thought of the mayhem the three girls could cause.

But that'd be nice though, huh? The three women you love most in the world getting to know each other?

He smiled at that. It *would* be nice. "I suppose I could introduce you."

Reaching inside her jacket, she pulled out a cream envelope, the address hand-written. *Dillon.* And he felt a lump form in his throat.

"I'm so glad that you know about Jason, Adam. And what Jess does, I-I'm glad it was them that told you. I suppose your broken leg, keeping you here in the bay, really has had a lot of positives..." A curious tone edged her voice, but she continued on. "But you finally knowing the truth about your sisters will make this a lot easier, than if I had to explain it all to you. It's from Dillon, I think you should read it."

The touch of the paper had flashes of Ireland leaping to mind, white flowers and miles of green and mist.

Grief cast its shadow across his heart.

Dear Lucy,

I've a few final matters to clear up, and I'm asking you to help me, even though I don't deserve it.

I don't want to reveal all the ugly things I've done; there have been many. Just know that in the last months I've made right those that I can. And those that I can't, I've tried to balance as best as I could.

I've used dark magic, Luce, and it's the balance of it that has been giving me the most worry.

I made a deal with the wrong sort, you see, and in repaying that debt I'm putting Adam's own flesh and blood in danger.

Despite all that I've done, he is a brother to me, and I wouldn't intentionally harm him or his kin any more than I would my own.

And so I need you to go to him. I sent him off in a rage, knowing he'd go to protect his sister, hoping that he could get to her in time. But now I need you to make sure it worked, make sure they're all safe.

The scourge are rising, they seek the chalice. Go to the wolf, don't be stubborn about it, you're going to need him.

Lay white tulips with Mama for me,
Love always,
Dillon.

"He's really gone." Adam leant his elbows on the table, resting his chin on his clasped hands. "Why didn't he come to us?"

Sadness had hollowed her out. He could see it so clearly now. Her smile was distant as she swirled her whisky, and absently stared out across the bay. "Would we have helped him? Either of us?" She took a sip, mulling the question, before turning that arresting gaze to him. "I don't think so. He'd run so far off the rails in these last few years."

Hindsight. What a bastard it was.

"But now, things are different. So here I am, doing what he asked. Are your sisters okay, Adam?"

Adam reached out, touching the paper, running his finger over Dillon's writing. His voice was sad but steady when he spoke. "Jess is here, in the bay. She had a run-in with a couple of vampires, more than once if I've pieced the whole story together right. She now has a full-time bodyguard in the shape of a werewolf who, from what I've seen, would gut anything that wanted to hurt her."

Unnameable emotion raced across Lucy's features at his

words, and the last lines of the letter played again in his mind. "Is that why Dillon wants you to go to Jason, for protection?"

Picking the letter up, she folded it, putting it back in her pocket. "I can protect myself."

Leaning back in his chair, Adam laced his fingers behind his head. He'd be buggered if he'd let them continue to keep him in the dark. "Luce, I've just had Jess glossing over the facts all afternoon. And I let it go, but only because I had nothing to bargain with. You on the other hand, need to tell me what's going on, or I won't tell you what I know." He grinned at her deadly stare. Ah, it felt like old times.

"Nice try, Adam, but there's nothing in this *situation* that you can help me with."

"Probably, I'm sure it doesn't matter anyway. After-all, I only had a quick chat with Jason and gave him something so he can track the vampire. I imagine he'll be updating you with what he's found, when you go to him. Right?"

Bingo.

Her eyes flared and her jaw set tight, at just the mention of Jason's name. And he allowed himself a moment's glee at getting on over on her.

Leaning forward he gave her a brotherly pat on the knee, and a wink. "Now, would you like to talk about it?"

"I swear, if you aren't the most irritating individual."

He shouted with laughter as she picked up her glass, downing the contents, before pushing to her feet on a sigh.

"Okay, you want full disclosure huh?"

Rubbing his hand down his face, he scraped his stubbled jaw. Gods', he needed to clean up his act. "Come on, Luce, I may've been the patronising king of trying to protect everyone with secrets, but look where it's got me." He swept his hand towards his leg. "Show a little pity, I've got to face both my sisters this week. And there's gonna be hell to pay."

Shrugging off her jacket, she hung it on the back of the

chair. And pulling a hairband out of her pocket, began to wrestle her fiery red hair into a messy topknot as she restlessly paced about.

"Well, I wish them well, as you've long had that coming." She shook her hands, like a boxer getting ready for a fight. "Right then, you think you can be brief? Pay attention."

She took him on a speeding race through the history of the Morrigan clan, explaining how their line were purposed with protecting and hiding the Ardagh Chalice. Vampires had used it in centuries past to resurrect powerful vampires, thus ensuring the continuation of the human-hunting breeds.

In her short concise history lesson, he learnt more about vampires than he ever needed to know. He also learnt that Dillon had revealed the location of the chalice to another clan, to entice a young pretty witch to have dinner with him.

"Vampires who feed on humanity have been, for centuries, known as The Scourge. And they have- a particularly bad history with the MacIntyre Pack."

"Jason's family?"

"Yes. Dillon knows that my power is more than strong enough to handle a single vampire, that I can see coming. But finding them is a different story. I can scry for vampires, the same as I can for the Chalice. But if they've been cloaked, I need a scent tracker. I don't need to find any vampires as long as I can locate and re-hide the chalice. But again, if it's mystically hidden, I still need a tracker..."

Adam sifted through everything she'd said. Before raising his brows. "So if you and Jason don't get along, which is the feeling I'm getting here, then just ask another MacIntyre?"

"I can't do that."

"Oh please,"—rolling his eyes, he held out his hands— "gimme a break. What aren't you saying, Luce?"

Her hands fisted at her sides as she whirled on him. "We're *fated*. He and I. It's written, or something equally bollocks. His pack won't help me, because *it's written* that I *have* to go to him."

The clock read 3am, and Adam could still hear Lucy pacing about in his spare room. Muttering and mumbling to herself.

He'd known her all these years, and he still couldn't believe she'd kept so much hidden.

As had he.

The upcoming *chat* with his sisters was stealing his sleep. Thoughts of Ellie lying warm and hot beneath him was making him sweat. Fear of the dream taking him back, leaving him lost and alone in the ocean kept him fearfully awake.

Normally the lack of control, and worry would be causing embers to lick his skin by now. But there was peace to be found in honesty.

Solace in truth.

His eyes drifted shut.

CHAPTER 8

BLONDE DOWNY HAIR *feathered around her sleeping face. The short locks looked like they would curl as they grew around her tiny head.*

Sarah stood silently looking into the crib, as the flames snapped in the hearth. The hisses and pops soothed her frayed nerves, and chased away the unusual chill being brought in by the damp summer night.

Thunder moaned in the distance. The storm was still miles out to sea, she had a little time yet. Time to burn these precious moments into her memory. To look at her daughter's sleeping face, and wonder what kind of woman she would grow into.

Sudden tears burnt her eyes, and hastily covering her mouth, she turned, stifling the sob that came from nowhere.

It would be so easy to run, she could take Althea and disappear into the night. Her mother had always told them they had a sister coven in Ireland. She could go, head east for Wales, and seek safe passage across the water.

But Althea was so small, and they couldn't make the distance before winter. And there was Eda... her sickness wasn't improving, and if she ran, the village would seek retribution against her sister.

'You walk this path alone. You must restore the balance.'

The words of the spirits settled across her. For magic to exist inside humanity, there must be balance, this she knew too well. She had used her magic to protect her own life during labour so that her daughter would live. And another gentle woman had paid the price.

She might have been able to right the wrong, given time. But the Fates would not wait, they demanded their due, and using David Thaine to reclaim their cup of blood was their answer.

Had it only been two days since they'd last met in the village? His sweet wife smiling tiredly, so full she'd been with child.

An agonising day later and he was alone in this world.

The pain and despair was choking.

She would not run.

But this burden, this terrible burden would end with her.

Three bottles sat before her. Three locks of hair. A roll of twine.

She placed a lock of hair to the neck of each bottle, and used the twine to secure it. Binding it around and around. Hair from Althea, Eda and herself.

She lifted the warm honeyed liquid from the fire, decanting it into a ceramic jug, before raising her hand above it.

She pierced her thumb with a needle, letting three drops of blood drip into the tonic. And whispered the spell by three.

> "You have your life, take my health.
> You have your life, take my health.
> You have your life, take my health."

The tonic fired with each drop, yellow lightening spearing through the liquid.

Lifting the jug she poured equal amounts into each bottle, pushed the stoppers into the necks. Then she stilled, holding her hands open.

> "A bottle for each,
> A bottle for all.
> A lock of hair from each,
> A lock of hair for all.

Once empty,
Seal these bottles and let them fall.
Into the ocean,
Into the tide,
Let the sea decide
Where the magic will hide.
Upon my last casting, let this spell be bound.
I will my sister Eda, to undertake my final
vow."

The bottles rattled and shook, as magic tolled in the air. It raced up the glass, carving curling patterns that sparked with power. Until the vibrating stopped, and stillness gripped the room.

The sudden noise cracked like the shattering of church windows, and Sarah fell back. Icy wind whipped through her, pulling her hair and clothes. It doused the fire, plunging the barn into darkness.

The voice of the spirits fell silent.

Relighting the fire, she laid protection on Althea, and placed the bottles in a sack.

It was time.

He came to, slowly, blinking heavy eyes.

Pushing his hair back from his face, he touched the sides of his head again. Wiping away the tracks of tears that had fallen.

Thea better hurry and get home. He had so much to tell them.

Turning onto his side, he met Murphy's sooty eyed gaze, as he sat patiently, watching. "Morning Murph, and how did our guest sleep?"

With nothing more than a solemn look, Murphy perfectly related his feelings; he was convinced neither of them knew what they were doing.

"That well, huh?"

Easing to sit at the side of the bed, he grabbed the boot, strapping his leg into it.

Shrugging into his heavy blue dressing gown he tied it up as he walked down the hall, to find the spare room empty. The bed was made, curtains drawn, and a note sat on the duvet.

Got some things to take care of, but I'll be about. Phone me if you need me.

BTW, I want an invite to Christmas.

L xx

He grinned, shoving the note in his pocket, before looking out the window towards the shore, squinting at the light.

He frowned as he stood there, the sun didn't make it round this side of the house till afternoon...

Disorientated, he shuffled around, checking the clock on the dresser.

One o'clock.

"What the hell?"

He'd slept thirteen hours!

"Murph you should've sat on me or something. Bloody-hell, have you had breakfast?"

The smarmy grin had Adam pinching the top of his nose. "You and herself cleared me out, didn't you?"

～

ELLIE LAY STILL. The sunlight was bright, the November day was cold. The sky was high and blindingly blue.

She'd made an early start. More of an enforced start, since sleep had evaded her most of the night. At six she'd given in, got dressed and walked down to the activity centre. She'd set up for the day, started the paperwork and waited for the Cutters to arrive.

They were taking potential new members out on the water today. She didn't envy the rowers in these freezing temperatures, not one bit.

She'd been alone for a whole day. And she still had no more of a clue as to what the hell was happening than yesterday. She'd been convinced that if she could just get some space, it would all make sense. All her ducks would start to line up.

Fat chance.

All she'd done was slip into auto-pilot. Stepped back into *regular* life, if there was any such thing. She'd driven around for a bit, turned up early for the meeting with two of her staff, and come home in a daze. Dinner, bath and bed.

And she'd lain there, for hours. Managing fitful, fretful sleep in-between.

After handing over the centre's keys to the coxswain, she'd locked her office and come home to stand in a hot shower. She hadn't been warm for days, not since yelling at him in the ocean.

You were pretty hot when Adam was wrapped around you.

"Oh shut it." Freshly showered, in comfy black leggings and a huge red and black chambray shirt, she'd flaked out on the bed, pulling the furry grey comforter from the foot of the bed over her legs.

He'd only been back in the bay since summer. Back in her life for three days, and she'd already fallen into his bed.

She'd also had her best friend apologise for avoiding her, come face to face with a werewolf, and, rather foolishly, assumed that Adam's dream of a vampire was symbolic. Because vampires didn't exist anymore...

Stopping her aimless staring out of the window, she rolled her eyes to the ceiling instead.

It didn't need to make sense. Lots of things in life didn't. She just needed to process it.

What you need to do is tell Thea the truth.

She sighed at the voice of her conscience. "True enough, and I will, as soon as she's back."

Shimmying off the bed, she straightened the comforter, and wandered downstairs. Telling Thea that she'd woken up all their magic would set some of this confusion to rights.

Being honest with Thea and Jess had to be dealt with first. She owed them the truth.

Then she could focus on her biggest problem: Adam.

She opened the fridge door.

Sod werewolves and vampires not being extinct.

That took care of itself with or without her knowing. But Adam, on the other hand. She just couldn't escape him, even when he wasn't bloody here!

Slamming the door she leant against the kitchen side, crossing her arms sulkily over her body. There were no answers in the fridge either.

"There's nothing at all in there."

Thoroughly disgusted with herself, she huffed into the hall. Pulling on her fur-lined calf boots, she dug about in the under the stairs cupboard for her quilted black coat, and thick red scarf.

Stopping to glance quickly in the hallway mirror, she ran a comb through her hair, and applied a dash of lipstick.

"It'll have to do."

The late-afternoon breeze was cutting, and Ellie gasped as it hit her.

Locking the door, she looked down the High Street towards the pub. She needed food, and people. She was accomplishing nothing, sat at home being mardy.

The tide was up, and the sun would be set soon enough.

The odd pumpkin still sat on doorsteps. One particularly

eager beaver had a little wooden Christmas tree sat in their window.

Hadn't it just been summer? Like seriously.

She frowned at the Christmas tree, then at herself. Before letting out another sigh. Gods' she needed to get over this mood.

A group of four walkers banged their boots as she stopped outside the pub, one of them already weighing up the chicken and leek pie or the lasagne. Ellie could attest to both being excellent.

She smiled at the woman, as she waited for them to go in. "They're both delicious, but the pie is served with an amazing wholegrain mustard mash if that helps sway you?"

The windswept walker groaned, "That sounds wonderful! I swear they've walked us from West Sussex, and we've earnt this, haven't we, Lindy?"

Their playful banter swept over her, and she felt herself begin to settle as she clicked the old door shut behind her. Maybe she'd sneak into the kitchen, have a cuppa and a chat with Lisa while she cooked the afternoon service.

Expecting to meet the cheerful face of Steve the landlord, Lisa's husband, across the bar, she stuttered to find Adam chatting with him.

Murphy came immediately to his feet, rushing to greet her.

If it wasn't for Murph, she might've been able to do a quick about-face and escape without being seen. But no such luck.

"Ellie!" Steve grinned. "What a day for visitors. Jess and her fella were in, you've just missed them." He splayed his hands on the bar, giving a wink

towards both her and Adam. "Mind you, they were being all lovey-dovey at the table in the corner, so maybe for the best."

Her voice was high and a little overwhelmed when she spoke. "Oh, I just popped in to catch Lisa." She pointed to the staff entrance that lead to the kitchen, still hoping to extricate herself.

Murphy pushed his smooth head back into her hand, as if demanding she stay, and planted his bum firmly beside her, leaning into her leg.

"Well, you're out of luck, she's been training up our new starter for a while now, and it's his first stint running the kitchen on his own. Lisa has left the building."

Ellie new Lisa had been trying to get someone to take on some of the cheffing, but of all the crummy timing. "Not to worry, I'll catch up with her later." Shame, she needed some peopling.

Adam had come to his feet in the narrow bar, his hand settled on her elbow, forcing her to look at him, to acknowledge him.

"Stay."

Adam's invitation was friendly and genuine, and she almost had to double-take. "No really, I—"

"I was going to have an early dinner, test the new chef." He threw a nod a Steve. "I hate to eat alone."

A small grumble sounded from Murphy's direction, and Ellie found herself smirking down at him. "I think Murph's trying to tell you something."

Giving him a rye look, he shook his head. "I mean it, stay and have some dinner. Lord knows there's nothing to eat at yours." His brows were raised, his blue eyes bright with amusement, and Ellie found she didn't know what to do with a 'Charming Adam.'

He looked... different.

"Great, the table by the fire is still free, I suggest you two grab it before someone else does. Ellie, I'll bring you a drink."

Steve rolled in, taking any chance she had of wrangling her way out it, and she found herself mutely agreeing.

How did she get herself into these things?

Murphy seemed to grin at her, before wandering off to lay behind the bar with Max.

Adam rose from the bar stool, gesturing her ahead of him, and she had no option but to walk the short distance to the little round table.

"You still look chilled. Wanna sit by the fire?"

Charming and polite. This is not how things worked between them, this *new* Adam, made her jumpy.

This is how he treats everyone.

"But not me."

"What's that?"

Crap, plastering on a smile, she shook her head. "Nothing, just nothing. And yes, fireside would be... nice."

She stood awkwardly as he moved behind her, her brows raised in question.

"Your coat, I'll take it."

Get a grip, woman!

"Of course. Sorry. I mean, thank you." *Oh, this is going well. Very well.*

Cursing her own ridiculousness, she pulled off her scarf and undid the large zipper on her quilted coat.

His hand took the collar, the tips of his fingers brushed her neck. He slid the coat down her arms as a shiver raced up her spine, and her cheeks heated.

Quickly seating herself, the roaring fire warmed her back, and it was then that she got a few moments to study him, as he went to hang her coat.

He was different. He was wearing jeans. The slim design allowed him to fasten the boot over the top. He wore a beaten up, brown, lace-up, ankle boot on his good leg. A close fitting grey grandad top moulded to his impressive shape. Reminding her anew how it had felt to have her hands on him, and she balled her fists in response.

The heavy duty watch and brown belt finished it off. He hadn't shaved, but had tidied up the growth. It suited him, and as he came back to the table the scent of delectable after-shave attacked her senses.

He looked fantastic; capable and more confident than he had in these last few days.

"You're looking good." Dammit! 'Well'. She'd meant to say well!

Bollocks, bollocks, bollocks.

His laugh was filled with surprise. "Thanks."

Heat flooded her cheeks, and her temperature spiked. "I meant—"

"Too late, no take backs." Grinning, he crossed his arms on the table, and leant towards her. "If it makes you feel any better. You always look good, and it was you who inspired me to have a bit more self-respect actually."

"It was?" She had absolutely no idea what to do or what to say. It was different when they'd been tearing off to find Jess, and *dealing* with the whole situation. But now, he was being all funny and kind. And she didn't know where she stood anymore.

He'd gone on the charm offensive, and she feared she just didn't have the willpower to hold him off.

"Sure, there you were yesterday, all pretty and pressed and put together. And I felt as used-up as old teabags, and I needed to snap out of it, you know? This damn leg, among other things," he gave her a long look that spoke volumes, "has knocked me for six. But I've done all the things that have brought me to this place, so, I gotta face the conse-quences and keep moving forward."

Truly amazed at his acceptance, she sat for a minute,

digesting all he'd said, as the young barmaid put a glass of red in front of her.

"You've, ah, come a long way in twenty four hours?" She sipped, making a mental note to self, that she'd only have one more. She was quite capable of throwing herself at him, and begging him to finish what they'd started yesterday morning, without the assistance of red wine. Thank you very much.

The fire behind her reflected in his blue eyes. The glow lit his features, making him look, impossibly, more handsome than he did to her already.

He pushed the sleeves of his top up his forearms, the light hair dusted his tanned skin. The open neck revealed his collar bone, and she stared at his jawline, wanting to put her lips there. She could spend hours just looking at him. It simply wasn't fair.

"I meant what I said before, I'm done with how things were between us. Things have changed."

This was her chance, to get things on an even footing between them. "You're right, they have. And you and I being better with each other will be so much better for everyone, what with all the things we have to discuss." She turned the glass between her hands, trying to make sure she was being clear. "It's not just you that has truths to admit to Thea and Jess, and us being civil will help this whole... situation." Finally looking at him straight on, it still disconcerted her to see no animosity in his gaze.

Taking a swallow from his pint, his mouth tipped in a lopsided smile. "'Civil' huh? Is that what we are?"

Ignoring the urge to pick up her glass to kill time, while she floundered about for an answer, she took a breath. *Crunch time, what are you going to say now?*

"I don't know." *Ain't that the truth.*

The fire backlit her perfectly, catching all the copper tones of dark brown hair. It hung in heavy waves, framing her heart-shaped face. Her pretty blue eyes were solemn and serious as she answered him.

He wanted to see her laugh and smile. At him.

He wanted to watch them flutter closed as he pressed into her...

The oversize red and black check shirt she wore, was loosely buttoned over a tight black top of some sort. The collar slipped towards one shoulder revealing a smooth expanse of golden skin.

She looked cosy and Christmassy today, and he wanted to unwrap her.

Hours of dream-free, healing sleep had been a boon. And gods' knew he should've noticed the pattern sooner, but he was slowly coming to realise that each time he corrected himself, or made right a misdemeanour from his past, his leg felt stronger.

When he'd lost his rag and shouted at Lucy it had pounded like the venom of a thousand snake bites.

And sitting across from Ellie now, everything felt right. Like it always had. But he'd used all the anger and bitterness to avoid facing how drawn he was to her. He'd blamed her for things she couldn't have possibly changed.

It was like the fog had lifted, he sailed just about everywhere, but always with her in his thoughts. And she'd been right here.

"Well, we're not strangers, or acquaintances. So where does that leave us?"

Her fingers fiddled with the stem of the wine glass. She had petite hands. Slim, rose gold bangles encircled her wrist.

He'd prefer to get her out of the pub and back to his, where he didn't have to put up with interruptions of others.

"Have you decided yet?"

Lifting his gaze to find Steve stood at the table, he was struck by the irony of his thoughts.

"I'm a creature of habit, so, steak for me. Ells?"

She visibly relaxed at the interruption, her shoulders losing their tension, her smile reaching her eyes as she turned to his friend.

"I was raving about the pie earlier, have you got any left?"

Steve jotted their order down on his pad. "Absolutely. Adam, where have you parked? You know the tide could end up in the High Street if the wind picks up, right?"

"No worries, I'm round the back."

Ellie looked questioningly at him as Steve left them. "You're driving?"

He rubbed the thigh muscle of his left leg, still unable to believe he hadn't figured out sooner that making things right was healing his leg. "Yeah, not my car though. I've pinched Thea's, it's an automatic.

My balance hasn't been up to it before, the thigh has been giving me jip, and unable to take any weight." He shrugged off revealing everything. "But time and a bloody good night's sleep have helped. Not to mention a change of attitude." He tipped his glass towards her. "And you."

She tensed up again, and he shook his head. "Ells, am I making you uncomfortable?"

"Yes." Her answer was instant, quickly followed by her covering her mouth.

He laughed at her stunned expression.

"Sorry, I didn't mean to blurt it. And not uncomfortable exactly. It's just, this is new. And I know you're like this with everyone. Else. But us being *friends* is going to take some getting used to."

"I want to be more than your friend, Ellie." He was sure his intentions were clear in his eyes, but his gaze dropped to her lips as they formed a whispered 'oh.'

High colour crested her cheek bones and the air changed

around them. Awareness flooded her gaze, and the sexual tension was so thick he was sure he could touch it.

Dammit, they both had friends here, he couldn't very well drag her out before they'd eaten.

"What about you, Ellie? Don't you want to be more than my *friend*?"

His heart pounded in his chest, he knew she wanted him. The pull between them had always been strong. But had he done too much damage? He wanted her, all of her. What if she said no...

Her teeth worked her bottom lip, and he almost groaned. Her breaths were shallow, the rise and fall of her bust, the way her fingers traced nervous circles on the table, all made him ache.

They couldn't leave anyway, the fitted jeans left him nowhere to hide, so getting up currently wasn't an option.

"I-I'm not sure that's a good idea."

He had to lean forward to catch her quiet words, and unconsciously cupped his hand around hers, his thumb laying on the inside of her wrist, rubbing her pulse.

It was erratic beneath his fingertip.

He shifted uncomfortably in his seat, and she made a strangled sound, at his laughter.

"What? You make me hot, and these jeans are cutting off some serious circulation."

"Adam!" she clearly didn't know whether to laugh or tell him off, but the visible tension in her frame eased as she released a sigh and a half laugh.

She picked up her wine, and took a sip. Leaving her other hand in his. The wine left a sheen on her lips as she spoke. "It would be pointless to deny that I'm attracted to you." She raised her brows at him. "But there's been so much anger between us, it'd be foolish to think a quick tumble would put all that right."

Ah, she was going for logic. Sensible he supposed. But then, it wasn't a 'no'. He slid his thumb from her wrist to her palm, and softly circled there. "I wasn't thinking of a 'quick' anything, Ells. And all I can hear is you not saying no."

She wrinkled her nose at him, as she reached for a response. And although he couldn't believe it, and knew he didn't deserve it, he knew she wasn't going to deny him.

"It's not about yes or no. We've only been talking for a few days."

He caught sight of the waitress approaching with their plates, and lowered his voice so only she could hear. "What's gone on between us was my fault. But tonight, I'm going to make it up to you."

Her pupils dilated at his words, and he prayed he could remember everything he'd ever heard, tried, seen or read, as the waitress set their food down with a smile.

"So eat up, you'll be needing your strength."

Her laughter surprised him, as he picked up a chip. "What's so funny?"

Laying her napkin on her lap, she shook her head. "You conceited ass. I'm almost inclined to let you try."

He grinned at her, he liked this between them. "Whatever excuse you need to give yourself. But I'll have you begging before the witching hour."

The banter was fun, but it was still making him hot, and judging by the energy pulsating between them, it was her too.

"Had a lot of practice then?" Her brow arched haughtily, as she pursed her lips primly, curiosity in her gaze.

"Nah, I just learn fast... but go slow, if you know what I mean."

The exaggerated leer he gave her made something akin to a giggle fall from her lips, and she inwardly cringed at how easy she was.

Who was she kidding? She was prepared to make the

most of this change of tide. If he was on the menu, she was ordering him to go.

She could've been mauled by a werewolf this week alone. Life was just too short.

And she really, really wanted to let him *make it up* to her.

She wasn't rubbish when it came to men. She just had no sense when it came to this man.

"Oh that's sleazy." She finished her wine, still flushed with pleasure at having him smile and laugh with her.

"How's your steak?" Steve placed his hand on Adam's shoulder as he came up behind him.

"Not as good as Lisa's, but don't tell the chef."

"Cheeky bugger. I'll send drinks over." He picked up hers and Adam's empty glasses as he moved on, checking in on other diners.

The food was delicious, the fire, the company. It was like the planets had aligned, and Ellie couldn't help but wonder how this evening had just fallen into place.

Murph drifted over in time to guilt Adam out of his last piece of steak, before taking a position in front of the fire.

And Ellie sipped her wine, answering his questions about the activity centre.

"I knew I wanted to come back to the bay after Uni, but I couldn't have imagined being able to start a business straight away."

"So how did you? I remember it just being a rundown old building, that needed knocking down."

"A developer wanted to buy it, and privatise that section of beach. I was still finishing my last year when it started, so don't remember all the initial hoo-ha. But there was a lot of kick back from the bay residents, but also the locals from Warblington village. Privatising the beach would deny them access."

"A developer, huh? That sounds pretty grand for our little

bay. What was it for?" He pushed his empty plate aside, and placed his elbow on the table.

He looked genuinely interested, but the further she'd got through her dinner the more conscious she was that she'd all but said she'd take him home.

Her throat dried, and she battened the nerves down. She wasn't going to fall at the last hurdle. No-one lit a fire in her like him.

"A private boat club. But it never came to that. My Dad got chatting with the local councilor who said it needed redeveloping by someone who would keep public access to the beach, and who had the local community's interest at heart. Dad got the idea for Stoney-Bay, and I took it from there."

"And now you're a self-made woman."

She laughed at that, but let the admiration in his eyes warm her. "With a midnight paperwork problem."

"The curse of being a business owner." He gestured to her empty glass. "Would you like another drink?"

She didn't want another drink, or a coffee, but was she ready to go? Had he been serious, and if he was, was she? "Well..."

"Come on, we'll have one back at mine." Sliding back his chair, he weaved through the now-packed pub, to get their coats, and she sat. More than a little shell-shocked. His house?

He waved across the lounge bar to Steve, who had hands loaded with plates, and mouthed, 'Put it on my tab.'

With a firm nod, a smile and a 'no worries,' he pushed through the swing door into the kitchen.

Adam held her coat.

So here it was, they were leaving. Together.

CHAPTER 9

HE OPENED the back door of Thea's little hatchback, for Murphy to jump in. Silently promising to get it cleaned before he gave it back. Shutting the door, he found Ellie looking at him.

"I've never been in your house." Her quiet words carried on the cold night air. The moonless sky was dark, and her breath lifted in plumes.

Without answer, he walked to her, cupping her face in his warm hands, and brushed his lips over her full ones. "I know. That's why we're going to remedy it, right now."

Opening the door, he waited until she was seated before going to the driver's side.

Murphy stayed quiet in the back, as Adam drove them onto the Island.

It felt good to be self-sufficient again. To have Ellie beside him.

He could feel her nerves, they matched his own, but this was right. He was sure down to his bones.

The roads were Saturday-night-busy, and headlights dashed across them. She hadn't said a word on the journey, and as they drove down his road and pulled onto the drive, he didn't cut the engine, but turned to her in the front seat. "It's okay if you've changed your mind."

At her slightly stricken look, he tucked her hair behind her ear, and stroked her cheek. His smile was self-deprecating as he said, "I know I haven't. But if you don't want this Ellie, that's fine." He winked at her. "But I'm gonna keep chancing my arm. You won't get rid of me that easily."

Her eyes lost their starkness as she looked at him. "I want you."

The breath lodged in his throat, and heat curled up his spine. Sliding his hand into her hair, he ever-so-gently eased her to him, so he could sample her sweet lips.

She tasted of wine and a woman's unique mysteriousness. The strands of her hair were winter cold, slipping through his fingers.

Breaking the kiss he stopped, her gaze was hot and sultry.

"I haven't made-out in a cold car since I was a teenager, and thank gods' now we don't have to. Come on, woman. That was your last chance."

He let Murphy out, and reached for her hand, wrapping it in his as he pulled her from the car.

Clicking the front door shut behind him, he caught Murphy sneaking off upstairs, taking himself out of the way. *Good lad.*

He hung their coats on the bannister, and led her into his home. Turning on the floor lights in the kitchen, he let the warm glow seep into the open plan living room Ellie stood on the rug in front of the fireplace, the ocean, visible from the large window, spread out behind her.

Grateful that he'd had the forethought to lay the fire before he'd gone out, he gave her a sly smile, and flung his hand at the grate. It roared to life, snapping as the dry kindling caught.

Closing some of the distance between them, she tilted her head to look up at him, humour glittering in her eyes. "Clever. But you're not the only witch I know."

He chuckled, and hooked his finger into the front of her shirt, tugging her closer. "I'd better learn some new tricks then."

He kissed her smile, wrapping his arm around her waist, drawing her fully to him.

Her hair brushed his arm as he tipped her back, taking playful kisses, before grazing his stubbled jaw up her neck.

He felt her breath catch, and did it again, loving the helpless little sound she made, as she held onto him.

Her hand trembled as she laid it on the back of his neck. Her nails lightly scraped his scalp, and the shudder rippled across his shoulders, as she let her head fall back.

Mouthing the column of her throat, her heated summery scent was strong there. He breathed it in, and settled his lips just under her ear, making the kisses butterfly soft. She softened, melting in his hold, and he took her down to the rug.

Her hair spilled around her, and he straddled her hips.

Reaching for the band of his top, he pulled it over his head, flinging it onto the chair behind him.

Her sigh was audible, and her hands flew up to touch him. The same as before, she traced his chest, her teeth worrying her bottom lip as her heavy eyes seemed to feast on his body.

Following the line of muscles across his stomach her breathing became hectic, and she reached for the button fly of his jeans.

He offered a silent thank you to the heavens for all the sit-ups and push-ups he did to keep the rage at bay. The flare of desire in her eyes was worth every punishing minute.

But he couldn't let her rush him. Stilling her hands, he held her wrists, laying them either side of her head. Kissing her lips, as he bent over her. "I can't let you do that, Baby."

Her kiss was carnal, hot and wet, and he knew he wouldn't last five minutes before plunging into her.

Murmuring low, he stroked her wrists in turn, excited beyond compare to watch his gold magic encircle them, pinning her where she was.

Her eyes flared wide when she tried to move, colour flooded her chest, travelling up her neck. The unconscious lift of her hips beneath him told him all he needed to know.

Her breathy sighs filled him.

"I want to apologise properly, Ellie..." His fingers shook as he worked to open each button of her shirt, until it fell away from her body.

The strapless black crop top cut a swathe across her, and although he desperately wanted to see her full breasts he knew he had to wait.

Kneeling beside her, he eased off her boots and leggings, leaving her in dark lacy briefs.

The light of the fire swept across her, as she lay like an offering for a god.

But she was no sacrifice, he was going to tend her, sate her, fill her. Until she could think of nothing but him.

He heard his own moan of anticipation at the sight of the bounty that lay before him.

Hooking his fingers each side of her crop top, he slowly, ever-so-slowly, pulled it down. Revealing her breasts one delectable inch at time.

Shutting his eyes tightly against the beauty of her nipples, he kept sliding the fabric down, until he reached her hips, taking her briefs too.

He focused on her shapely thighs, knees, calves and ankles, finally sweeping the garments away.

Unable to deny himself any longer he knelt back to look at her.

Arms spread, breasts high, full hips. She'd arched her back

from the floor, lifting her breasts higher still, the nipples hard, waiting for him.

"Adam..." She moaned his name, low and long, and he was stunned. Dazzled by her. His very own Aphrodite, resplendent, bathed by fire.

"Ellie." He could barely say her name as he came down over her, taking her lips, pressing his chest against her.

Gods', the feel of her. He wanted her to know how beautiful she was.

Re-straddling her hips, the denim of his jeans rubbed her soft flesh, drawing a gasp from her, and then another as he slid his hands beneath her back, cradling her.

He smoothed his stubbled jaw over the full curve of her breast, the nipple, revelling in her whimper. He waited a beat, and placed the softest kiss on the hard nub, causing her to arch as high as she could from the rug, pushing herself towards him. Until finally he wrapped his lips around the nipple, drawing it into his mouth.

He worked his tongue across her as he sucked, and her gasps ran in time with his rhythmic pulls. He laved her breasts, holding the weight of her while he bent over her in homage. Until she was nothing more than a continuous moan, her skin wet and shiny in the dancing light.

Her head tossed and turned, her hips lifting into him, and he gritted his teeth against the urge to grip her hips and push into her.

But he wanted more, needed to experience all of her.

Easing between her legs, he rubbed his cheek against her stomach, caressing the curve of her hips, grasping the tops of her thighs, asking her to open further. Trust him further.

The sight of her nearly broke him, her tender lips, and smooth, smooth skin. He pressed a long kiss, high on the inside of her thigh. And soaked up the shuddering moan that rippled through her, before touching his tongue to the very core of her.

She was wet and lush, and he groaned against her, as her own sweet, high cry reached his ears.

Gripping her hips, he clamped his eyes shut, consciously slowing his breaths, consciously slowing down, so he didn't just fall on her, madly.

Easy now.

Her leg slid smoothly over his shoulder, across his back, and he wondered if the price would be his sanity.

Her hips moved with a hypnotic sway, as if to lure him closer. Who was he to deny her?

She tasted exquisite, and with each lick she quaked beneath him, until his name was a litany on her lips.

This. He was lost.

Fumbling with the buttons on his jeans, he freed himself, rising above her, to take her lips. Kiss her jaw. Whisper.

"Ellie, baby, I..." He choked as she opened lustrous eyes to look at him. The ocean swirled in her luminous gaze, and she lifted her lips for his kiss, her lids closing.

"Now, Adam. Now."

Her heat slipped across him as she arched up, and he moaned at her wetness bathing his length. "So good."

Leaning his weight on his forearms, he circled his hips, nudging the head into her sheath. She was so tight.

He stilled above her, breathing harshly, her lashes fluttered as her eyes opened to look up at him.

"Ellie?" Too tight.

She tightened and flexed her inner muscles around the tip of him, and he couldn't help but push deeper.

Her breath caught, and her eyes glazed, and he stared down at her, stunned.

The solid length of him was gripped tight, and she moved again, forcing him deeper. "Gods! Ellie!" His shout lifted above them, and he was, all at once, in one last thrust, packed fully inside her.

She trembled around him, and he held rigidly still, glorying in the wonder of her, and equally horrified that he'd hurt her. "Ellie?"

Her breath sighed out, her smile tremulous. Her eyes sparkled. "Yes?"

"You're a—" He couldn't say the word as he caught sight of her wrists, still bound by his magic.

"Jesus, let me." He rubbed his hands across the bindings, freeing her. Unable to understand her throaty laugh, or the way her arms so readily wrapped around his shoulders, her fingers shifting through his hair.

"I was. But now I'm not." She had the look of a siren as she pulled him down, kissing his lips. "Aren't you going to finish making me beg?"

Heat crawled across his cheeks at the thought of what he'd done to her. "Ellie, I'm sorry—"

She cut him off. "I'm not," and lifted her legs, so he sank deeper. Pulling moans from both of them.

Wrapping her legs around his hips, she arched her hips slowly, as if testing this new feeling.

His eyes damn near rolled back in his head. The sweet depth of her was delicious, and he just couldn't leave her heat.

"Ah, baby." He answered her shy hip-roll with one of his own, loving the surprise in her eyes when he stayed tightly in her, to grind low.

Lust raced up and down his spine, and he moaned against her lips, sweeping his tongue deeply into her mouth.

She crossed her ankles, locking him tighter to her, and he rewarded her with another hot, heavy grind against her throbbing core.

Her cries were thin and high and he couldn't stop himself from wringing them from her, until she flung her arms above her head and came in scalding rush, dousing him. He thrust deep into her, losing his very breath as he filled her with everything he had.

The fire had burned low when he'd finally regained his composure enough to carefully ease away from her. And still her arms made to pull him back with a whispered, "Don't go."

"I'm not, but we'll freeze if we stay here." The side of her facing away from the fire had already started to chill.

Coming clumsily to all fours, and then his knees, her snuffled laughter had him looking up. "Funny huh?"

His jeans were jammed around his thighs, coupled with the boot around his left leg, he was in serious danger of ending up flat on his face if he tried to stand.

"It certainly reveals some of your more *interesting* parts."

"Oh, give over." Going back to his hands and knees, he then lay flat on his chest, and turned onto his back, pulling up his jeans. Before rolling over again, and pushing to his feet, reaching down a hand to pull her to hers.

Taking her chin between his thumb and forefinger, he tipped her face for a kiss, and deliberately catching her off guard, swung her up into his arms, shirt and all.

"Adam! You'll break the pair of us if you try and carry me anywhere."

Looking down at her, he grinned. "Wasn't going to."

He felt strong, fully balanced and in control. For the first time in months.

Magic coursed through him, and with her warm against his chest, he hazed across the room to the stairs, and then again, into his bedroom.

The power snapped through him, pure and true.

And he let the feeling of rightness sweep through him, before setting her to her feet. "There now, isn't that better."

Ellie pushed her hair back from her face, a slight look of

embarrassment in her eyes, as she pulled her unbuttoned shirt around her.

"Hey now, don't cover those pretty breasts." He made to tug at the shirt, letting her slap at his hands with a laugh. "Would you like a t-shirt to sleep in?"

She tucked her hair behind her ear, in a delightful gesture he was coming to recognise she did, when feeling bashful or shy.

Pulling a plain t-shirt from his drawer, he held it towards her, waiting for her to take it before saying. "Not that I was intending to let you sleep much, but you can keep it nearby, I s'pose."

She tipped her head, and her brow. "Oh really. Turn around, please."

Closing the distance between them, he held her waist, nuzzling his stubble up her neck in the way she seemed to like. Loving the way her breath caught. "As adorable as you are, you don't need to hide from me. Here."

Taking the t-shirt he tucked it beneath his arm, placing a hot, sucking kiss on the sensitive skin between her shoulder and neck, teasing the shirt off her shoulders as he did so.

She tipped her head, her hair dropping away, and he trailed across her jaw to her lips.

They were already swollen from his kisses, and he stepped back, pulling the t-shirt over her head, smoothing it down her body.

His hands settled on her hips, and he couldn't put off asking her. "Did I hurt you?"

She smoothed her palm across his chest, running her finger down the centre, making him shiver. "It was worth a little pain. And I heal. Fast."

Grabbing her hand he pulled her across the room. "Then come to bed, woman."

Murphy's bark snapped Adam's eyes open, and he met Ellie's gaze at point blank range. Looking equally startled.

By the sounds of the noise Murphy had gone rattling downstairs, which made more sense as the doorbell rang.

"Oh gods!" Ellie sat-up, pulling at the array of pillows and covers tangled around her.

Enjoying the view, he folded his arms behind his head. "Whatcha doing?"

"I'm looking for,"—she came up from leaning over the side of the bed, flicking her hair everywhere, holding the t-shirt like a trophy—"the t-shirt. Who's at the door?"

Her voice was a squeak, and he laughed at the look of horror on her face. "Dunno. Don't worry about it, they'll go away."

The very distinct sound of a key in the lock, had Ellie's look sliding into nauseated, as Jess's voice echoed through the ground floor. "Adam?"

"Ah, shit. She used her key."

He started to push off the bed, when Ellie lunged for him, grabbing his face in her hands. Whispering desperately. "Don't tell her I'm here!"

He scrunched his face at that. "Why the hell not?"

"Shhh! I mean it, please, Adam." Tears filled her eyes, and he instantly took her shoulders, rubbing her arms.

"Hey, why so upset, it's only Jess."

"I know, but please. We all have so much to talk about, and I have things to explain too, and... and, just please."

Shaking his head in bewilderment, he agreed. "Okay, okay, just hold on."

Raising his voice, he called down the stairs. "I'm getting dressed, make me a coffee and I'll be down."

Her muttering about him being a lazy arse floated up the stairs, and he huffed at his sister.

"Just stay up here then." Pulling on his jeans, he strapped

on the boot. Briefly noticing how much healthier his leg was looking. "If you change your mind, come on down. It'll be fine."

She pulled the duvet right up to her shoulders, and sat scrunched against the headboard. "I know, I know, but I just want to get the big stuff sorted. And I'm all... and we've been, you know." Hot colour flooded her face, as she looked at him, and he couldn't help but grin down at her.

"You're pretty when you're embarrassed, Ellie Thaine."

With a scowled 'oh,' she pulled the blanket over her head.

And he laughed as he walked away.

Standing on the landing, he considered the dog-leg stairwell, and shrugged. Jess was already onto him, so he hazed down, and then down again.

"Well, well. Aren't you throwing caution to the wind? Thea can do that without having to see where she's going, y'know."

He ignored his sister's irreverent greeting, and went to open the patio doors for Murphy to take himself outside.

She was reaching into the fridge as he turned round, and he quickly grabbed Ellie's clothes and his top from the arm chair, and dropped them behind the sofa on his way past.

"I take it from that, that you can't do either. So I'll be asking Thea to walk me through how she does it then." He arched his brow as he took the coffee from her. "And what do you want at this time of the morning?"

"And you're obviously feeling more chipper than you were." Jess casually looked around him into the living room. "I wonder what's caused such a change of mood?" She sipped her coffee, and when she realised he wasn't going to answer, she rolled her eyes. "Fine. And it's 11am, I thought you were an early riser?"

"Sleep heals, and all that."

Her noncommittal 'hmmmm' wasn't lost on him. She always liked to nosey into things. Little brat that she was.

Giving in, he grinned at her. "Come on, Jessica, what's the emergency?"

She laughed outright at his use of her full name. "Thea got back late yesterday, don't you check your phone? Anyways, she's cooking Sunday roast—thank the gods—as Seb can *eat*. And I think it's time we all talked."

He felt the slight buzz of energy down his leg at her words, and knew it was time. "Sounds good, what time shall I be there?"

Jess leant nonchalantly against the side as she sipped her tea. "She's sent me out to hunter gather at the supermarket, and we couldn't get hold of you or Ellie, so I'm making the rounds. Lunch is at two."

"Okay then, well you'd better finish your tea and get a move on." As her brows raised in question, he turned to let Murphy in. "You know how Thea likes to have everything before she starts. And don't worry about Ellie, I'll let her know."

"Oh you will, will you? So you two really have buried your top-secret-hatchet then?"

Ellie all but squeaked as she leapt away from where she'd been eavesdropping, hanging over the bannister. Backing into his bedroom, she ever-so-carefully pushed the door to. "Dammit, dammit, dammit!"

She tugged at the hem of his t-shirt, and caught sight of her reflection in his full length mirror.

She looked like she'd been rolling around all night.

You bloody have!

Tutting at her little voice, she took a closer look.

Her hair was *everywhere* and as she caught sight of her legs, she stared in shock at the red whisker marks on her inner thighs.

She flushed clear to the roots of her hair, and whirled away from the mirror, before turning back. She touched one of the marks, and granted herself a secret smile, as a flash of her begging his name bounced through her mind.

They'd made love, all night. And it had been glorious.

"And just what are you doing?"

With a leap and a screech, she clutched her pounding heart to find him stood in the doorway. "Adam, why are you sneaking about?!"

He dumped their clothes on the foot of the bed, and stalked, boot and all, towards her as he saw her legs. "I marked you."

His expression was murderous as he went to his knees before her, running his hands up the outside of her thighs, his thumbs carefully tracing the marks.

"Adam." She made to step away, and he merely secured her with a hand on her waist. "It's fine, it's nothing."

"It's not nothing. I marked your skin."

Heat poured through her, as she looked down at him on his knees before her. "Yes you did." Her voice sounded husky to her ears. "I think I may have marked you too." She remembered digging her nails into his hips, and his groan as he'd tried not to plunge too deep.

His blue eyes dilated as he looked up at her, and she found her hand on his jaw, the other slipping into his hair, his arms tightening around her waist.

"Ellie…" His low murmur of her name had her pulse jumping, as did Murphy's footsteps on the stairs.

Wriggling from his embrace, she backed away. "Now you stay over there." She held her hand up as he came to his feet. "I mean it, this is how these things start in the first place. What did Jess say?"

He slowed his steps towards her at the mention of his

sister's name. "Not much, I told her I'd let you know, and we'd meet them at Mill House just before two o'clock."

She opened her mouth to question him some more, but he stopped her.

"Na-ah. I don't know what she thought was going on—other than me sleeping late—but she did not think you were hiding up here."

Crossing her arms indignantly, she lifted her chin. "I wasn't hiding."

"Yeah, right."

"Fine, maybe I was. But I just want to get on with this, whatever we're calling it."

CHAPTER 10

Summit. This is a Summit Meeting.

Ellie swallowed nervously as Marc met her on the drive. She hugged him tightly, "I'm sorry you had to cut your trip to Mum and Dad's short."

He squeezed her arms as he stepped back. "We're going to head back up again soon, don't worry. And this is important." Giving her a look of brotherly concern, he looked over his shoulder, he seemed to be making sure they were alone. "Are you okay? I'm going to be having a quiet word with Adam about the London thing, now, don't stop me. I know you and he don't get along, but I won't have you put in harm's way Ellie. And neither will Thea."

Rolling her eyes skyward, she huffed. "Marc don't be daft. I wouldn't stand by and let anything happen to Jess any more than you would. Also, I can take care of myself." She held her hands up to stop him interrupting her. "And Adam and I have worked it out."

Marc pursed his lips at that. "Have you now?"

"Yes, what with all the Jess goings-on, it put us in the right position to... er... put the past behind us." She pointedly ignored stumbling over her words, before nodding at the house. "Now can we go in? It's freezing out here." The cold hadn't let up, and she had no doubt the bitter afternoon would drop to heavy frosts by nightfall.

Following him down the drive, she saw everyone's cars already here, including Adam's.

She checked her scarf was properly folded around her. Grateful that she'd convinced him to drop her home, so that she could change. And more importantly, so they could arrive separately.

She just wasn't ready to face all the questions, she didn't even know what they were doing or what it all meant. *You could just ask him.* Another tut. All she did was tut at her stupid little voice.

The last thing she needed was her well-meaning best friends and brother getting involved.

Poppy and Murphy scrambled across the room, to see who could greet her first, and she took precious minutes to soak up their joy, and stroke soft heads and ears.

To find herself being wrapped up by Thea. Her beautifully calming energy instantly taking the edge off her nerves. "Glad you're back."

Thea's brown eyes were serious as she looked at Ellie. "I'm glad you're here. No thanks to my idiot brother."

Adam's groan from behind them, had Ellie tensing. "Thea, there's no blame here. We just went to help Jess."

"That's kind of you to try and protect him Ells, but he's on the block for this. If he'd been honest with Jess and I in the first place, maybe this all wouldn't be happening."

Ellie physically felt Adam's sadness at Thea's words, and she just couldn't let him take the blame. "There's more than one person keeping secrets, Thea. I've been keeping things too." She took a deep breath, and looked at her best friend squarely. "I'm the reason your magic came back, everything you went through in the beginning, Thea, was all because of me."

Four pairs of stunned eyes, and assorted 'what?'s settled on her.

She kept her head up, they were entitled to shout and scream if they wanted to. Ellie just hoped she was strong enough to take it.

It was then that she felt the comforting warmth of Adam's hand on her lower back, as he came to stand beside her. "I'd say we've kicked this little *meeting* off, wouldn't you?" he addressed the room at large, rubbing her back before turning to her. "Let's have your coat."

It seemed like no one was going to tell her to leave, so she unzipped her quilted coat, handing it to Adam with a smile that was all lip service.

He seemed to be back by her side in seconds, gesturing her towards the large kitchen table, which looked out over the bay.

After she'd sat, he seated himself beside her and looked over at the others. "If you want to come and sit, we'll tell you how we met, and explain why the magic came back."

Ellie caught Thea's confused glance to Jess, as Jess pushed to her feet and headed over. "This I've got to hear."

As they gathered, and took their seats around her, Ellie haltingly began to explain how she'd sailed out into the bay one hot day in August.

Murphy came to sit between her and Adam, laying his head in her lap. She stroked his smooth ears as she spoke, looking to Adam to fill in here and there, until finally she finished. "But somehow, I woke Adam's magic, and by the time we started back at Uni you were in a terrible state. I didn't know he was your brother, and by the time it came to light it was too late to explain. Or maybe I was just too afraid. But Jess always seemed to be fine, and I couldn't put it together. Then you and I moved home, Thea, and I got to know Jess, and she was fine. Maybe it's because you were younger—you'd had time to adjust?" She looked questioningly at Jess, before hanging her head. "I just don't know."

She took a calming breath, lifting her eyes from the table. "I'm so sorry."

Silence met her words. Shocked faces, and silence.

Adam made-out he was stroking Murphy's head under the table, but grabbed her hand, giving her a squeeze before letting go.

"And I blamed Ellie." He shook his head, and laid his clasped hands on the table. "Nan had spent my life telling me that my 'power would be worth the struggle in the end' and I didn't want it—the power, or the struggle. And so I've proceeded to spend that last seven years treating Ellie like a complete bastard, because I blamed her. And she took it, because she loves both of you." He looked between both of his sisters. "So there it is. Part one, I suppose."

"Well," Jess crossed her arms, and leant back in her chair, "if you think part two belongs to you, Adam, you've got another think coming. Because, holy crap, you two are crackers!"

"Jess..." Thea rubbed her forehead, rolling her eyes. "They're trying to explain."

On a huff, she flicked back her long dark hair. "I know that, but bloody hell, Thea, a chunk of this could've all been avoided if these two dolts had just talked to either of us!"

"How are we in the firing line? Especially not Ellie, she's just tried to do the right thing all a-bloody-long, and I've made her life miserable for it."

Intending to point out that he wasn't as special as he thought he was, Ellie never got a word in, as Jess and Adam were now fully bickering across the table.

Seb merely waited her out, as if he found the whole thing

amusing, while Marc glared silently at Adam like he might like to throw him in the oggin.

Ellie mutely looked to Thea to sort them out. The slightest glitter of humour lingered in her gaze, and she winked at Ellie as if they shared a secret. Where was the anger, the blame?

Thea slowly rubbed her hands together, before pointing sharply at her brother and sister. The zap had them both jerking in their seats, with Jess turning to her sister. "Hey!"

"Shut it. Both of you." Releasing remaining sparks to ether she murmured to herself. "Could've so done with that when we were teenagers." Before clearing her throat. "Jess is right I—" She sent Jess a sharp look to keep it zipped so she could finish. "In the fact that the 'part two' is ours. She also has a god point; if either of you had just come to either of us, we could've straightened this out pretty-much on the spot."

"Ellie, you didn't 'wake' my magic up, or Jess's. Only Adam's. And you didn't wake it, you were just the nearest magical source for it to latch on to." Ellie pointedly looked over the table, down at Murphy. "And the one sat between you two, trying to look innocent, probably picked up Ellie's signature a mile away."

Ellie and Adam both looked down, shocked, to find Murphy looking distantly out to the bay, avoiding eye contact.

"Jess, why don't you go first?"

Jess had taken Seb's hand in hers, cradling it on her lap. "What Thea and I have come to understand in the last few years..." she looked pointedly at her brother, "...by talking,"— he merely waved her on—"...is that it was time to for the magic to wake up. We think Nan helped that along as much as she could. There was no stopping it. In fact, it actively sought out what it needed; a jumpstart from another person of power, or being that was *other*."

Ellie frowned at that. "A jumpstart? When I tried to heal Adam's head I felt something then, like it was taking what it needed."

Jess nodded. "Exactly, and it was. You couldn't possibly have triggered all of us, just by charging Adam's magic, you'd have needed to heal all three of us, individually, when we were in our BM state. That's 'before magic' to you Adam. Which you would know, had you bothered to talk with us."

Adam glared at Jess. "Now listen—"

"No, not again. Just get on with it, Jess." Thea glared at him as she spoke, and he scrunched his nose at her.

"So if Ellie didn't pizazz your magic, then what the hell did?" Adam leant across the table.

"Jason."

The energy in the room shifted, and Adam was clearly aware that Seb was having some control issues of his own.

"My magic wanted out, it was earlier than you or Thea, June time I think, and Jason hadn't made his first change. That's the thing with our magic, it wasn't prepared to wait, it knew what it needed and it created situations to get us there. Jason's brothers had shifted to wolf form and were running the sandbanks in the middle of the night, trying to help him make his first shift. And I'd decided that Nan didn't know what she was talking about, and I was going to go and watch the sunrise. I'd walked round the coast road at low tide, got stuck as the tide rushed back in, and literally fell over Jase mid-shift. Totally enough energy there to launch rockets, let alone magic. Anyway, I raced home, and crawled into bed. Convinced I was hallucinating, and that I'd poisoned myself on some flower or herb, and fell asleep. I had a nightmare, and the magic woke me. I was touching the ceiling. Bang, magical Jess."

"Of all the..." Adam pushed his chair back, pacing awkwardly away. Conscious that his leg was throbbing, he tried as best as he could to temper his voice, before turning back. He didn't quite manage it. "You could've been bloody killed!"

"Hmmm, that happens when in dangerous situations, doesn't it?" Jess gave him a flat look. "What really happened to your leg?"

He opened his mouth.

Closed it.

And sat back down. "Fine. Point made."

It was going to grate on his last nerve to tell them everything, but even just that slight admittance had lessened his aching leg a hundred-fold.

"What did happen?"

"I want to hear about Thea." He sighed. "Then I'll tell you. I'll answer whatever you want to ask."

Jess whistled low at his quiet statement, "Thea, make it quick."

On a short laugh, she opened her hands. "Oh, mine is simple. Nan was narked that I was racing around living like a Londoner, when she knew I belonged here in the bay." She smiled warmly at Marc, and Adam felt a contented rush at her obvious happiness. "So she sent me a parcel. It was a deck of tarot cards; old ones, thrumming with family magic. Handed down through the Lavelles, from about the mid-eighteen hundreds so Jess can tell. It wasn't enough to do the whole job, but it woke enough to make me feel like crap for a few months. Then I went back to Uni and Ellie was able to do the rest." Thea clasped Ellie's hand. "I had no idea you'd thought you were to blame. If it wasn't for you, I'd still be stuck in that cycle of overwhelm, not knowing which way was up."

As he'd listened to Thea, every word was another kick. He owed Ellie more than an apology. He should get down on his knees and bloody beg for forgiveness.

"Those early months of my magic not being fully online, had kind of programmed me really, not to trust it. Not to trust myself. But once I got back here, things started to click into place. But of course, by then, you and Jess had started treating me with kid gloves, and you'd gone off gallivanting with the navy."

"I wasn't in the navy."

The stark admission produced yet more stunned silence. Even Ellie had turned to him, her hand covering her mouth.

"Then why did you leave?" It was Thea's distress that hurt him the most, the worry on her face.

"I wanted to protect you, I was angry and raging. I thought if I could just find a way to get rid of the magic..."

The words, the past, all came tumbling out; Ireland and Dillon, how he'd thought he was missing something and he and Dillon's spell had almost fried him. How he dreamed, but it was blanking them out, because they'd blocked him, and so he was never able to fully understand the warnings.

And it was like a balm, to finally share his struggle. "And that's how I knew you were in trouble, Jess, Dillon called me."

He fell silent, not sure what to say to the pale faces looking back at him. Until Ellie spoke quietly. "Tell them all of it. Don't protect them, tell them, Adam."

He hung his head. "And it's when I can't control situations, like when I can protect you two, that the rage. It... uh... gets out of hand, and I can't switch it off." He cleared his throat, before continuing. "That's why I try and stay close to, or even on, the ocean." His laugh was self-deprecating.

"As it stops the worst of the burning until I've calmed down."

With a gasp of horror Thea raced to him, wrapping her arms around him. Before he knew what was happening, Jess was there too. His guardians, his flesh and blood who loved him no matter how big a jerk he'd been.

He felt tears prick his eyes, and he crouched awkwardly, trying to hug them back. But it was hard when you were sat down, being mothered.

Jess wiped her tears, and pulled a tissue from her pocket, handing it to him. "Sometimes. Adam. I swear..."

"Love you too." He swallowed passed the lump in his throat, taking Thea's hand. Her face lined with horror at his story. "Thea, don't, I'm—"

"Don't you dare tell me you are fine! You are most certainly not *fine.*"

"But I am, I'm doing better honest, ask Ellie."

Jess and Thea turned on her, hands on hips, warrior-women ready to fight for their blood. *Is he doing better?*

"Adam, define better?"

"I am better, Ells, tell them. I haven't had a rage since that night on the beach, that's what, four, five days ago now. And when I did have a wobble you stopped it. See; better."

Ellie felt her throat dry. "How often were you having the rages before, if four or five days is *good?*"

"As long as I stayed away from trouble, or on the water, longer. But once the dreams about the bottles, and being stranded, well..." he lowered his voice, "most days."

Ellie covered her trembling cry with her hands. Tears springing to her eyes at all the pain he'd been suffering. "Oh Adam, no."

Her tears seemed to galvanise everyone. Before she knew it, she'd been ushered to the couch, with warm jasmine tea. Adam had been ordered to sit with her, while Thea rushed round the kitchen, checking the dinner. And Jess paced about, seemingly working through the whole situation.

With a sudden snap of her fingers, she pointed at Adam,

and pulled the little foot stool over, sitting in front of them. "What bottles? Why are you dreaming about bottles?"

On a sigh, Adam braced his hands on his knees. "It doesn't much matter now. But there are three bottles, from when the magic was bound. When Thea said that our ancestor had told her about the bottles, I brushed it off, because I didn't want to... well, I didn't want either of you to get in harm's way looking for them, when I already was. But you both need your magic now, and I can't find the bottles, so it doesn't matter. But one is protected by something savage off the coast of Myrina... hence the leg. And the other two are lost or hidden, as I can't locate them."

Thea had walked closer as she'd listened, placing her hand on Jess's shoulder. "Oh gods, Adam."

Thea went and pulled a sturdy wooden box from the bookshelf. She set it on the kitchen table, and waved her hand across the charmed clasp, opening it. Jess came to stand by her, and they held their hands over it. Chanting.

Magic danced around him, motes of green and lavender, and he watched in amazement as Thea, then Jess reached elbow deep into the small box, and produced... two blue apothecary bottles. Miniature bolts of lightning traced the engravings, as they set them down on the table, and Thea turned to him. "We hid them. Not from you, but from every-one. I found this one in the reclaimers yard, on The Island during the summer, and Jess, well, as it turns out, she'd had hers all along. Nan left it to her. But we only put it all together after Sarah's ghostly visit."

"So the other one is in the ocean?"

At Jess's quiet question, he nodded. "But it's not for us now. I'm sure of it. I dreamed I walked into your office, and the bottles were on your board. And one is lying down, murky and faded." He shook his head. "We're not supposed to give the magic back. No matter what I thought when I went tearing off years ago. You need your magic."

"But we won't stand by and let you burn." Thea's bare statement was laced with pain, and he couldn't stand it.

"But I'm not. And I won't, or I don't think I will, not as long as I don't keep secrets or try to keep you both in the dark."

Marc placed his hands carefully on Thea's shoulders, hugging her back against him. "Here now. We can't solve this in one day. It's been three hundred years in the making. But you've all come further this afternoon than you have in seven years."

Adam nodded gratefully at Marc. "He's right, Thea. We've come this far, and I'm not going anywhere, I want to see this through."

Jess ruffled his hair, like she used to when they were kids, and he'd chase her all over the house. As Thea nodded, with a sad smile.

"Okay. Then I suppose we better eat, before the pork dries out to dust. And in the coming days, we'll find a way to sort this out. Once and for all."

Ellie stayed mostly quiet through dinner. The sun had set, and the temperature plummeted as she'd known it would. They laughed and chatted as the day moved into evening, and Ellie was content to join in when needed. But she was mostly waiting for her chance to leave.

To walk home in the quiet night air, and try and clear her mind. To regroup.

She found her chance when Adam went to help Marc get wood for the fire. He needed time with his family now.

She pulled Thea aside, hugged her tight, whispering that she needed five minutes peace.

"Of course, whatever you need."

Thea walked her out through the patio doors, so she could go unnoticed.

"Say good night to Marc and everyone. Thank you for sneaking me out." Her eyes filled with a fresh rush of tears, and she laughed at her overemotional self. "Love you, Thea."

Wiping her own eyes, Thea tugged a lock of Ellie's hair. "Love you too, now go and get some rest, and that's an order."

The air was clean and cool as she breathed it in. It lifted all the negative, making her feel refreshed and clear headed again.

She hadn't forced Adam's magic on him as they'd both thought. But she couldn't blame him; she'd kept her secret for years. If she'd explained it to Thea in the beginning maybe this could've all been avoided.

Both she and he carried blame in this. And in the end their secrets had only hurt them.

Turning the key in the latch, she moved through her quiet home. Turning on the hallway light, she set the thermostat and headed upstairs. Sleep.

Shedding her clothes, she pulled on her cotton shorts and tank top, and crawled into bed. The shiver from the cold sheets was welcome, and she smiled as her head touched the pillow. But in the darkness, she looked across the empty expanse of bed, and wished that Adam looked back at her. His blue eyes had watched her so intently, his hands had touched her with such purpose.

Sitting up in bed, she let the aching loneliness wash over.

Getting up she walked the hallway to the room where he'd slept, and picked up his pillow. It smelled like him, and she rubbed her face into the cotton, taking it back to her room and dropping it on the bed.

On a whim, she went to the top of the stairs, confused when headlights shone.

quay, until the wind died down and we could get it out of the water."

"It's a good job I was here then."

Giving him a sly grin, she walked towards him. The easy sway of her hips in skinny jeans, briefly seized his attention, and he made sure to slide his hands around them when she got close enough, pulling her between his spread legs.

"I'm not denying that, but what *are* you doing here?"

Busying himself with the feel of her lush curves beneath his palms, and inhaling the feminine scent at her neck, he patted her arse. "Thea wants me to pop in before lunch, she has a theory on a casting that might bind the burning inside me."

Wriggling, she pushed at his shoulders, leaning back. "That's great! What are you waiting for, go talk with her."

Angling her lower body back to him, he grinned. "Thought I'd come and get you first. And we could go together. You know, together-together."

He watched her closely, unable to decipher why she was still putting off telling anyone that they were seeing each other.

Sneaking around might be some people's idea of fun. But it wasn't his.

"Come on, Ells, what's this all about? I can't even hold your hand. Hell, at this point it'd be nice just to arrive and leave with you."

Shaking her head, she firmly extricated herself from his hold. "I know, and I know you think I'm nuts. But it's only been a little while, and this is so new between us. It's nice that it's just *ours* for now. Jess and Seb will be back on their mental schedules in a few days, and Thea will be back to work and everything will... calm down."

"Okay, a few more days won't kill me. Are you sure you don't want to come to Thea's?"

"Go, go and spend time with them, I've got mountains of work to do here, and if I don't get it done now, I'll have to work this evening and then I won't be free for... other things."

His kiss was deep and hot, a promise of those *other things*. "Well then, I suggest you crack on."

He kissed her once more, and headed for the door. "Going to grab a few things, then go to Thea's. Text me when you're done."

"Will do." She watched him go, the fine view of him walking away was not to be missed.

He seemed so relaxed, more than she'd ever known him to be.

She sighed as her eyes followed him until he was out of sight. They couldn't tell Thea and Jess, not yet. She knew her friends would be all over of him about what his 'intentions' were, and she cringed at the thought.

They both knew that she'd never been involved, which meant Thea had most likely told Marc, and that would cause of whole special kind of hassle. She loved them all dearly, but everything had got so complicated. Adam only just had his family back, the last thing he needed was pressure from them to... to...

What? Make a commitment?

Oh gods, it had only been a couple of weeks. They needed time to just be together.

And you want him to choose you without interference from them.

"Yes." The miserable word left her lips, and she stared down at the pile of junior sign up forms.

Picking up a pen, she read the first name three times before it registered, and thanked the gods when her mobile rang.

"Hey Jess, what's up?"

Excitement danced across the line. "Can you go to Mill House?"

"Um, yeah sure. Why?"

"No. No questions, just go now, I'll see you there in ten, and don't tell Thea I called, okay?"

Jess's laughter was infectious, and intrigued, Ellie found herself laughing in return. "Okay. I'm going, right now."

Grabbing her bag and jacket, she scribbled a quick note for the head instructor of the day, and locked the office door.

She zipped up the windbreaker as she hurried along the beach towards her parents' house, where Marc and Thea lived most of the time now. It looked like she would be seeing Adam this afternoon, after all.

Aided by the gusting wind, she was all but pushed round the curving wall along the path.

Latching the gate open, knowing Jess would be minutes behind her, Ellie hurried down the drive and rang the bell.

"Ellie!" Thea gestured her in from the cold, "I was just saying to Marc I wondered if we'd see you today. Adam'll be here in a bit." Her smile was wide as she took her coat.

"Will he?" The question sounded inanely weak even to her own ears.

At the sound of a car, Thea nodded. "That must be him now."

Ellie skirted round Thea and headed into the house, leaving Adam to deal with Thea.

"Hey, thought I'd see you today." The twinkle in her brother's eye didn't help either.

"So I heard." Brushing non-existent crumbs from her jeans, she was happy that at least Poppy didn't seem to be laughing at her. She pranced around Ellie's legs, and Ellie couldn't help but grin down at the pretty labrador.

"Put the kettle on, Ells, I'll go see what's going on."

Stroking Poppy's velvety face, Ellie spoke to her. "I should've stuck with dogs, shouldn't I, Poppy, huh? None of this human business."

As she mooched around the kitchen, the commotion spilled in from the hallway.

Thea pulled a glowing Jess along behind her. "Ells, look!" Jess brandished a dazzling sapphire.

"Jess!" Elation erupted within her, and Ellie sped across the room.

Ellie found herself wrapped in a hug filled with tears and laughter. These women, were everything to her.

Taking Jess's hand, Thea and Ellie took a moment to look at the sapphire, wrapped in an ornate gold twist. "OhMy-Gosh, Jess, it's beautiful, and perfect."

Happy tears tracked down Jess's face, and Ellie smiled at her. "This was soooo worth leaving work for."

With a shout of laughter, Jess squeezed her cheek to Ellie's. "You'd better believe it."

Adam, Seb and Marc had clearly done their, much more low-key, congratulating, and had set out six crystal tumblers.

Boxes of Christmas decorations were half opened around them, and Ellie felt her heart swell at the sight of these wonderful people.

Her fingers brushed Adam's as he passed her a glass, and she smiled at him. She was being an idiot. She wanted him, and hiding their relationship from everyone wasn't going to save her from hurt, if he eventually decided he didn't want her back.

Seb raised his glass, and the happy chatter quietened.

"To change. It brings us what we need most."

As their glasses met, Ellie knew the flash of magic as the crystal touched was a very good thing, and she laughed as the sparks flashed like tiny fireworks.

"Perfect." Adam's arm was warm pressed against hers, and Ellie felt her heart would burst. The whiskey buzzed on her tongue and sizzled all the way down, and she gasped as its warmth spread through her.

"And now all we have to do is plan it. She's only giving us a matter of weeks!"

Thea's slightly panicked voice, had Jess guiltily smiling. "It's true, my closest humans, Christmas Eve, and here in the bay."

"I'm getting notepads, we need lists, people."

Marc groaned as Thea dashed to the study, and Ellie laughed. The ringing of her mobile, had her guiltily smiling too, as she checked the caller ID. "It's work, just give me a minute." She hurried into the hall, rapidly explaining that it was fine for them to finish early if the winds had picked up. "But I won't be back today, we've got major good news here. If I text you the alarm sequence, could you set it for me?"

"You're a star." Hanging up on her head instructor, she leant against the wall, able to see Adam's back as she started typing the alarm sequence.

He had on those slim jeans today, and she took a moment to admire the fine way they fitted him, before shaking herself back to the task at hand, as their words drifted over her.

"And I know it's soon, Thea. But don't panic; I thought we'd keep it to just the seven of us: me and Seb, you and Marc, Jason, Adam and Ellie."

"Can we add one more?"

At Adam's words Ellie lifted her head, wondering who on earth he'd like to bring to such an intimate occasion.

"You, ah, want to bring someone to the wedding?" Even Thea's voice sounded confused.

Ellie watched, her heart plummeting as he rubbed his hand across the back of his neck, like he did when he was feeling uncomfortable.

"Yeah. She's... ah, really important to me, and I'd like you all to meet her."

She...

She found herself stepping back, until the wall stopped her.

Ellie just couldn't process what he was saying.

He was still talking, telling them about *her*.

She needed to get out.

Now.

She couldn't...

Staring down at the phone in her hands, she didn't send the text. Just turned off her phone and turned away.

"You'd like us to meet a *special female* in your life—who's not already in this house?" Adam caught the look Jess threw Thea.

"Jess." The warning tone in Thea's voice, was laced with concern, as she looked at Adam. "Does everyone here already know about this woman?"

Adam shook his head. "No. No it's not like that. She's Dillon's sister. What I never said about Dillon was his surname; it's O'Leary, and his sister, Lucy, is—"

"You're friends with Lucy O'Leary?" Jess's mouth hung wide as the incredulous words left her mouth. "You?"

"Ah, hell." His leg tingled and throbbed, in a way it hadn't for weeks. Running his fingers through his hair, he took a breath, determined to just get it all out there. "When I left the bay it was the O'Learys that kind of, took me in, you could say. And I, ah...I missed you both so much, and Lucy. Well, it was like having you around, she's like blood to me. And she's been dying to meet you for years, but I didn't want... And in the rest of this story I come off looking like a knob again, so there it is." He finished in a rush, turning to Jess. "It'd mean a lot to me, I *know* it's your wedding but I want you both to meet—"

Jess jumped to her feet, clapping her hands, as she threw her arms around him, and kissed his cheek. "No problemo. I'm a total fan girl of hers you know." Her eyes flickered from brown to lavender. "Oh, the things I've heard about her! She's one pow-er-ful witch."

"Is she single?" Seb's question had Jess turning on him, planting her hands on her hips, until she caught the gleam in his eye. "I was just thinking, we do have a little debt to settle."

A look of evil glee filled Jess's smile, as she feigned innocence. "Seb, you're such a good friend." She gave a little titter behind her hand.

Adam hid a smile of his own, it'd be nice to get a dig at the big bastard, and Lucy clearly wasn't going to do what was safest for her and ask for his help. "Oh she's single... her and Jase would be a good match, to my thinking."

"Oh matchmaking at a wedding. Isn't love grand?" Jess reclaimed her seat next to Seb, clearly thinking over all the variables.

"There's a lot of it about," said Thea with smirk. "Where *is* Ellie?"

At the mention of her name, the throbbing in his leg intensified, and he turned looking for her. "Ells?"

Marc walked through the house, into the hallway.

"Her coat and bag are gone, maybe a problem at work?" Marc frowned, taking his phone from his back pocket, calling her. "It's gone straight to answer machine, but it does if she's in the activity centre, it's a dead signal zone." His voice trailed away.

Adam was already pulling on his coat. She wouldn't have just left.

"Where are you going in such a hurry?" Thea raised her brows pointedly. "She's probably just popped back to lock up and she'll be back in a bit."

"No." Adam just shook his head, zipping up his coat, the rain had started to fall in earnest. "She's upset."

"And how would you know?" Thea came to her feet, and

Jess leant forward in her chair. Anticipation tinged the air, as his sisters waited for him. "Adam?"

"Well, she's here one minute and then she's not. Of course she's upset, or something, and we can't have that."

Thea nodded solemnly. "You're right, of course. But she's my best friend, and Marc's sister, we'll go and look for her."

"You certainly don't look like you're in much of a rush to go and find her, I'll go." His words came out in a frustrated rush as he walked towards the door. "Stay here, Murph, it's raining cats out there."

"Adam?" Thea's voice stopped him, and he looked furiously back at her. "Why are *you* in such a rush?"

"Well, I bloody love her, don't I! I can't have her running around in the rain, upset and on her own."

A chorus of cheers followed him as he slammed out of the house on a mutter. "Bloody sisters. Where are you, Ellie?"

She'd set the alarm at the centre, and walked along the beach, fat drops of rain, splatting against her windbreaker.

Tears dripped down her cheeks. Gods, she was such a fool.

He had an *important woman* in his life, and it wasn't her.

Who was so important that he needed his sisters to meet her? At Jess's wedding of all places?

She didn't bother to stifle the miserable sound that rung from her.

Everything had been so completely perfect, she'd looked across to find him looking back at her, and she'd wanted to stay in that moment forever.

But no, he was trading her out. She had obviously been fine to keep him entertained, but with an *important* family event like this, he wanted an *important* woman to share it with. And that wasn't her.

Climbing the steps she walked along the quay that lead through the marina. The windows of the boats where dark, all mostly moored up for the winter now. The sheets rattled hollowly, and the waves slapped the hulls.

Ellie just kept walking, watching her walking boots take one step after another. The wood beneath her feet shone, the guide lights reflecting the rain.

Her hair was wet and sticking to her head. The cold rain chilled her to the bone, and she came to standstill at the end of the last stretch of boardwalk.

The last few slips were empty, and the bay stretched out before her. The tide was winter-choppy, nothing to worry about.

What an inane thing to notice; choppy water.

But as she stood there, her mind shied away from anything else.

Adam was a gnawing ache in her heart, the pain consuming. Logical thought was something she just couldn't manage right now.

"Ells?"

The sound of his voice had her heart constricting in her chest, and her breath hitched on a sob, as she lifted her face, eyes closed, to the rainy night sky. "Go home."

"Ellie." His whisper of her name was accompanied by his warm hands settling on her shoulders, turning her towards him. "Baby, don't cry. I'm sorry if you felt like I was pressuring you to tell everyone about us."

Ellie kept her eyes closed, but dropped her head as he turned her around, she just didn't have the strength to push him away. She never had. "It doesn't matter now."

His arms were so wonderful as he eased her close to him. "It doesn't? That's good, because I may have told them..."

She moaned against his chest, shaking her head. "Now they'll know what a fool I was."

He was trying to tuck the wet strands of hair behind her ear. "A fool? Baby, you're freezing, let's go home."

"Nooooo." She buried the word into his soaking shirt. "Is she there?" Her words stuttered as she spoke,

"She? Ellie, Ells... who?" his words were softly exasperated.

"*Your important woman.*"

"My import... Oh lordy, Ellie. I didn't think you were listening."

"S-okay. Do you... d'you, love her?" Ellie couldn't understand why she was putting herself through this.

"No, Ells, I love you."

She struggled, trying to make him let her go, but he wouldn't, and angry tears bled in with the rain.

"Don't make fun of me as well as everything else!"

"Ellie—"

"No! It's fine if you don't, if you..."—her voice caught, the ball of emotion burning in her throat, but she pushed the words out—"...don't love me. But—"

"Ellie. The *other* woman, is Lucy O'Leary, she's like a sister to me." On a sigh, he touched his forehead to hers. "Ellie, she's Jason's life-mate, we're going to fix them up. I love you."

She frowned, trying to process what he was telling her. "You do?"

His laughter rumbled through her. "Well, I just shouted that I do at all our family and friends, so yeah, I love you."

"You did?"

"I did."

"Oh." She stood for a minute, a wash of emotion rushing around inside her, sniffing.

She looked down. She was crying and shouting and soaked to the skin.

"I... Oh gods!" She put the heels of her palms to her puffy eyes, embarrassment coursing through her. "I've made a total arse of myself."

His laughter rumbled through her some more. "You do seem to have your moments."

She blinked rapidly, as he repeated her own words back to her.

"Just in case you didn't hear me." His lips were hot when they touched hers. "I said, I love you."

She released a small laugh, "You'd have to, 'cause I'm a mad woman." Laying her hands on his chest, she tested the wet fabric. "And gods knows, I love you. In case this little episode wasn't enough to clue you in."

Her watery laugh was lost to his kiss, and as she wrapped her arms around him, touching his skin he jerked back. "Woman, you're freezing! I'm taking you home."

EPILOGUE

ELLIE WATCHED Jess and Sebastian sway together. Her dress was a fluted ivory column, and her long dark hair was a riot of curls, littered with tiny red flowers. She looked perfect.

"Thea, this place looks amazing—just perfect. I can't believe you got it all done."

Adam's hand took hers as he came to stand with her and his sister. "Ellie's right, Thea, everything is brilliant."

The huge spruce Christmas tree graced the lounge, with views of the bay behind, and pretty cream fairy lights dripped from the ceiling. Swathes of pine boughs, dressed with deep red velvet bows ran across the fireplace and windows.

The table had been laid with crisp white linen, and was buckling under the weight of all the food.

"Thanks, I've loved every minute of it. It's not every day that I get to host my sister's wedding." Thea's blonde curls had been pinned up high, spilling around her face, and the long midnight blue sheath she wore matched Ellie's. And Lucy's.

Squeezing Adam's hand, she gave him a quick wink and let him go.

Lucy had sidled out towards the kitchen, and seeing Jason frown in that general direction, Ellie figured she'd go and run interference.

"Hey."

"Ellie, well now, I haven't had chance to properly talk with you yet."

Lucy's rich brogue was a beautiful thing all on its own, and that was before coming face-to-face with the most arrestingly beautiful woman Ellie had ever laid eyes on.

"I saw Jason looking this way, and I thought you might like some company."

Her ready smile faltered at the mention of his name, and she lifted one shoulder. "Ah, so Adam's told you then?"

"Only me. And your secret is safe, and that's a promise."

"I heard you maybe thought, that I might be more to Adam. I can't help but feel I owe you some kind of apology, or something?"

Letting out the breath she hadn't been aware she was holding, Ellie made for the fridge, and pulled out one of the many bottles of champagne residing there.

"I can't deny, what with all the fuss on the run up to this shindig, and having no time to even squeeze in a quick 'hello' first, I was nervous about meeting you." Taking two champagne flutes from the cabinet and setting them down, Ellie wrapped the bottle in a linen tea towel and lifted the cork with a tiny pop. "But Adam was right, you're everything he said." Pouring the frothy liquid, she filled the flutes to the brim and handed one to Lucy. "To friends and family, old and new."

Her green eyes filmed with tears, and on a husky laugh she tapped her glass to Ellie's. "Well now, I'll drink to that."

"Not alone you won't." Jess stood in the archway, a glass of champagne in each hand, and Thea close behind her. "This is a toast for us girls."

Setting down her flute, Lucy riffled through her clutch. Pulling out her phone. "Then it's a moment we'll keep."

Taking her phone, Seb waved a hand. "Closer together then, Lovely Ladies."

Arms around waists, they laughed at the groom, and lifted their glasses after the photo was taken. But Ellie pressed the moment into her memory.

"So much for 'just the eight of us' then, Jess?" Ellie grinned at the bride.

"Just the eight of us for the important bit. But we couldn't keep all of Thea's hard work to ourselves, could we?"

Thea rolled her eyes at her sister, a silly grin ruining the effect.

Ellie had been overjoyed that her and Marc's parents had made it down, and that close friends from the bay had ventured out on Christmas Eve.

She knew she was walking on air, and smiling like a fool, but she didn't care.

Adam pulled out the bar stool next to Lucy at the breakfast bar, and set down his drink. "How you holding up?"

"Adam Thaine, if I didn't love you, I might murder you."

He let his laughter lift, happy to just be happy. He saw the way Lucy and Jason looked at each other, they both had it coming.

"And what about you, boyo, did you figure it out?"

Taking a sip he lifted a brow. "Figure what out?" A small smirk wreathed her pretty face and he squinted at her. "Come on, spill it."

"Your leg, and your magic. Did you figure it out?"

Elbow on the side, he perched his face on his hand. "My leg has healed, it seemed to be warning me to reveal the truth or suffer the consequences. And my magic? Thea thinks she's found a way to bind the fire."

At her slow nod, he frowned. "Why?"

"Well now, it's only my opinion, you understand. But the fire doesn't need binding, your magic needs finishing off. Which is all wrapped up in the creature that wanted to keep your bottle safely hidden at the bottom of the Aegean Sea."

Intrigued, Adam put his glass down. "You have my attention."

"Mermaids, like trinkets and keepsakes. But like all beings of power, they have to keep balance. I would say, that you went to fetch the bottle and she didn't want to give it up, even though it was rightfully yours. So, she corrected the imbalance."

"How did she do that?"

"By giving you what your heart desired most."

Lucy knew more about magic than he ever would, but even without her upbringing, he knew her intuition was her strongest asset, and that was saying something. "And I desired what... Ellie?"

Her laughter was lilting, and the downlights in the kitchen caused myriad colours to undulate through the plaits and twists in her hair. "Oh you men, you're funny. Yes, you *lusted* after her. But your heart, it yearned for your family, a home. It yearned for those you love to be happy, to be together. And I, especially, thank you kindly for that. You *wanted* rid of your magic, but it wasn't what you *needed*. Mermaids are rare; rarer than vampires, for that matter. Capricious creatures they are. But, this one had, to my thinking, kept something from you—the bottle—which in turn, caused you pain."

"So why would she give me all this, for a bottle?" Adam looked across the room; family, friends and the love of his life lay before his eyes. He'd give her all three bottles, and gladly.

"Think of the tarot, Adam. Water is the seat of all

emotion. And you must understand that mermaids are truly cursed. They long for love and companionship. She has something that you dearly wanted, were willing to risk your life for. The only thing she could give you greater, was that which she could not have. This. And the broken leg, that was just her way of making sure you didn't screw it up."

Lucy held up her flute. "You are a brave soul." She tipped her glass to him before taking a sip. "And if I were you, that witch whom you love—for she is a witch—I would let her finish healing you."

Smiling at his friend, he clasped her hand, and felt the lump in his throat threaten to halt his words. "Thank you." Lightly clearing his throat, he waved his hand, as she raised a brow at him. "Go on, tell me, I know you're dying to."

"You know me too well." She leaned towards him, and lowered her voice. "As I do you. The disclosure spell I cast was more than forth-coming. The witch, Sarah, changed the wording on her last casting as she burned. And magic is fickle; it didn't curse the Thaine's, it gave them a strain of Lavelle magic, so they might understand what she went through. The magic is what draws you together, the fact that you've all fallen in love is choice. They are your coven. And what you said the last time we were together, *'can you imagine if she'd actually finished?'* That's the thing, you need Ellie to finish what she started. You need her to heal you."

Adam drifted through the party in a daze. A mermaid. *What were the odds?*

Ellie was warm in his arms as they moved, the saxophone floating dreamily around them as they drifted together across the makeshift dance floor.

As the witching hour approached, the last few guests had drifted off. He knew his kin, his *coven* was close by. But all he needed right now was Ellie, liquid soft and wrapped in his arms.

Christmas lights starred his vision, Thea had scented pine cones in oils before throwing them the fire. And scents of orange and cinnamon teased the air. Never had Yule gifted him with so much.

But as he lay his cheek on her head, nuzzling her silky hair, he looked through the window and caught sight of the full Cold Moon in the freezing December sky.

You have faced your trials. Where do you wish to go from here?

The tender voice of the spirit world reached his ears, and he hesitated, tightening his embrace around his future.

He wanted to be whole.

"Ellie, come on." Taking her hand in his, she looked sleepily up at him. "I need you to do something for me."

He glanced over his shoulder, they were alone, had been edging to the furthest part of the house for some time. Now he knew why.

Unlocking the back door in the utility room, he tugged Ellie out onto the decking.

Her sharp intake of air, and sudden laugh fluttered around him. "It's truly bitter out here! Adam, what on earth?"

Continuing round the house, he brought her to a standstill in the darkness, on the large decked patio. The heavy drapes had been drawn across the study windows. And they faced out onto the ocean. The tide lapped the decking, and the moon speared across the water.

"Ellie. I want you to heal me."

Judging by the look on her face he couldn't have shocked her more.

"Adam, I-I will, always. But maybe today isn't the right time to try. It's been, ah... emotional? And wonderful. I don't think now is the time."

He grasped both her hands in his. He *knew*, soul deep, that this was right. "Ellie, I may not trust myself. But I do trust you. I'm asking you, please. Will you heal me?"

She closed her eyes, tears escaping, rolling down her cheeks as their breaths smoked and lifted into the night sky. The moon kissed the bare skin of her shoulders, as the strapless, midnight gown made her look like a true heathen.

Holding her hands before her, she drew a deep breath, and the very tide seemed to pull with her.

Stars and planets, galaxies and constellations spun in the light emanating from her palms as she stepped to him. "Are you sure?"

He felt his magic tremble within him, a sense of relief like he'd never known seemed to sigh around him. "It's time, Ellie."

Her static touch ricocheted through him, and power and magic chased up his veins. Ringing in his ears and pounding in his blood. It trilled in his system, coursing in his very bones. The bolt of energy hit him like lightning, and as he opened stunned eyes to Ellie's shocked ones, it flung him back, over the railing and into the sea, Ellie's scream of his name following him down.

Ellie raced to the railings, yanking up her dress as Seb and Jess, Thea and Marc, and Jason and Lucy poured out onto the decking.

"Oh gods, Adam!" Holding her long gown up around her thighs, she gripped the railings and vaulted into the dark, freezing ocean.

The water was icy, the waves batting her this way and that, as she kicked and swam for him. The dress tangled around her legs, he had disappeared from sight.

"Adam." She called out to the empty sky, Murphy's bark from the house echoed out behind her. And for a split second she caught a flash break the surface.

She kicked out for him. Diving down.

It was impossible to see beneath the waves, the water

seemed black, alien. And then she touched him; his hand grabbed hers tightly, and she dragged him and herself to the surface.

They broke through the waves, his voice a shout of triumph as he yanked her to him. His lips hot as they found hers.

Ellie sobbed for breath as she touched his face, his hair, his shoulders. "Adam, ohmygods, I'm sorry, I'm sorry, so sorry."

"Ells, Ellie. Stop." He kicked, supporting them as they bobbed in the waves, his hands sliding her legs around his hips. "Ellie." His final call of her name stopped her. The water heated around them, bubbled. The chill faded away and she looked into his eyes.

They sparkled blue and gold, and his smile was the one she knew. He'd warmed their small part of the sea, it fizzed and she couldn't help but reach out, touching the effervescence.

"I don't need the burning bound Ellie, I needed to trust that you could finish what you started."

A shout of laughter from the decking reached them as he spoke, as Lucy's voice called out. "There you go, boyo."

Ellie let the laughter bubble up, throwing her arm around his neck. "Don't you ever scare me like that again."

He gave her a wink. "No, ma'am."

Their oasis of warmth had been moving, on course, back to Mill House. Until finally, sets of hands reached over, pulling them from the briny deep.

The night air whipped at them, yanking any thought of warmth away, as they were hurried inside by those who loved them.

Towels and blankets were piled around them, but Ellie didn't mind.

Lucy ruffled Adam's hair, and had Thea laughing as she came forward to do the same. Ellie simply let them fuss over her, as she sat inside the curl of Adam's arm. But he seemed to be fidgeting. "What's the matter?"

Giving her an innocent look, he moved a bit more, seeming to untangle his way through the layers of blankets and towels, until finally he fought his way out and pushed to his feet.

"Ells." He straightened up, pulling at the wet shirt that stuck so wonderfully to his chest. "I've been carrying this for a while, just waiting."

Time seemed to freeze around her as he lowered to one knee.

"Marry me?" The pearl he held before her was wrapped in a coiled twist and Ellie couldn't speak past the wonder.

Pulling at the layers, she launched herself at him, burying her face into his neck.

His arms clamped round her, as he announced to the room. "I'm gonna take that as a yes."

Tears and laughter greeted him, along with one other voice.

"Ah, bloody hell."

Seven pairs of eyes watched Marc stalk to the tree, with Poppy at his heals. Half out of sight, he bent down, seemingly giving the adolescent Lab something. Until finally he moved away, and Poppy all but pranced across the room to Thea, obediently sitting before her.

She held a smooth black leather jewellery box in her mouth, and Marc shrugged awkwardly at the room. "We've been practising."

Tears already streamed down Thea's face as she took the box, opening it, to reveal an intricately carved, medieval gold ring, holding a ruby. "What do you say, Thea; will you marry me?"

Poppy's double bark had her laughing and crying as Marc went to her, sweeping her to him.

Ellie laughed softly in Adam's ear, "I'm so glad you broke your leg."

The End

COMING IN 2022, LUCY & JASON...

Joanne x
www.joannemallory.com

ABOUT THE AUTHOR

Joanne Mallory is wife, mother, and canine wrangler. She has always written, everything from poetry to historical papers. But at heart she's always been a romance girl... Romance with a dash of magic.

A history grad, who once managed a castle, she is always finding new things to try and new places to visit.

Joanne was born in Hampshire on the south coast of England, where she still lives with her noisy family, and foolish dogs.

To learn more you can find her at **www. joannemallory.com**

Printed in Great Britain
by Amazon